"DON'T BE AFRAID, ARIANNA. LET ME GUIDE YOU...."

Paul's lips were on hers, his tongue tickling the corner of her mouth. Then his lips claimed hers in a kiss that absorbed her whole being in the wild delight radiating from her mouth to her quivering body. His embrace was almost crushing, then it loosened and his hand slipped inside to caress her, sliding beneath the soft knit top to find her breast. A shiver traveled through Arianna that frightened and excited her even more. And then his kisses overcame all her will to resist....

SHARON WAGNER was born in Idaho, raised in northern Montana, and is now happily settled in Mesa, Arizona. An accomplished author, she started writing after college and to date has had some forty books published. She lives with her mother and two dogs, Muffin and Bitsy.

Dear Reader:

The editors of Rapture Romance have only one thing to say—thank you! At a time when there are so many books to choose from, you have welcomed ours with open arms, trying new authors, coming back again and again, and writing us of your enthusiasm. Frankly, we're thrilled!

In fact, the response has been so great that we now feel confident that you are ready for more stories which explore all the possibilities that exist when today's men and women fall in love. We are proud to announce that we will now be publishing four titles each month, because you've told us that two Rapture Romances simply aren't enough. Of course, we won't substitute quantity for quality! We will continue to select only the finest of sensual love stories, stories in which the passionate physical expression of love is the glorious culmination of the entire experience of falling in love.

And please keep writing to us! We love to hear from our readers, and we take your comments and opinions seriously. If you have a few minutes, we would appreciate your filling out the questionnaire at the back of this book, or feel free to write us at the address below. Some of our readers have asked how they can write to their favorite authors, and we applaud their thoughtfulness. Writers need to hear from their fans, and while we cannot give out addresses, we are more than happy to forward any mail.

Happy reading!

Robin Grunder
Rapture Romance
New American Library
1633 Broadway
New York, NY 10019

STRANGERS WHO LOVE

by

Sharon Wagner

RR

RAPTURE ROMANCE

NEW AMERICAN LIBRARY

TIMES MIRROR

To Domino,
whose encouragement and belief
give special meaning to the words
friendship and fan . . . with thanks

PUBLISHER'S NOTE

This novel is a work of fiction. Names, characters, places, and incidents either are the product of the author's imagination or are used fictitiously, and any resemblance to actual persons, living or dead, events, or locales is entirely coincidental.

Copyright © 1983 by Sharon Wagner

SIGNET, SIGNET CLASSIC, MENTOR, PLUME, MERIDIAN AND NAL BOOKS are published by The New American Library, Inc., 1633 Broadway, New York, New York 10019

First Printing, September, 1983

1 2 3 4 5 6 7 8 9

PRINTED IN THE UNITED STATES OF AMERICA

Chapter One

❧

Arianna sat rigid, holding her back straight with a concentrated effort of will. She wouldn't collapse now, she told herself. She had to be strong, had to face this second blow as she'd managed to endure the first.

"I'm sorry, Arianna," Mr. Potter murmured, his pale blue eyes compassionate. "I only wish there was someone who could help you through this sad time."

She allowed herself a slightly bitter smile. "Friends, you mean?"

"Someone close, to offer you emotional support," Mr. Potter said. He was a distinguished-looking attorney, but it was obvious to Arianna that he was finding this particular meeting slightly more trying than his usual efforts. "Losing your father so tragically was bad enough, but to have to face all this so soon afterward," he said, waving a languid hand at the papers that littered his dark wood desk.

" 'All this,' as you call it, has pretty well taken care of my friends." Arianna made the admission quietly, controlling the pain she still felt as she remembered the

way the consoling visits and phone calls had stopped
once the rumors of her father's poor financial condi-
tion had begun to circulate. She moved her head slightly
to ease the tension in her neck, and her shoulder-
length golden hair fell gently around her delicate
features, making her look younger than twenty-three.

Mr. Potter looked as though he might like to argue,
then simply sighed. "I will, of course, handle everything for you as I did for your father."

"From what you've just said, there isn't much for you
to take care of," she observed, lifting a slender hand to
smooth a wisp of hair back from her large brown eyes.

The agony of her father's death in a small plane
crash was still fresh, and today's revelation about his
financial problems had done nothing to ease her feelings.
Though Mr. Potter had assured her that the trust fund
her father had set up for her would be protected from
the general chaos, the realization that everything else
she'd known and loved would have to be sold to satisfy
the company debts was a second blow to her world.

For a moment Mr. Potter looked defensive. "I handled his legal work, Arianna," he reminded her, "not
the management of his financial empire. Though I
must tell you that, had he not . . . been lost, it is very
likely that he would have survived this particular money
crisis just as he did the ones in the past. He was a
genius."

Arianna said nothing, for her throat was closed with
the pain of her loss. Her father had been her whole
world for most of her life and now she wasn't sure
exactly how to go about building a future without his
advice and guidance. She got to her feet quickly, knock-

ing her purse to the floor and using it as an excuse to drop her head and avoid Mr. Potter's probing eyes.

"There is one more matter that I think needs your attention before you go," Mr. Potter told her, getting to his feet. "I'm not sure how you'll want it handled."

"What's that?" Arianna asked, perching herself on the edge of the chair. Better to face it all now, she told herself; she was too numb to feel any more pain.

"I came across this file when I was going through your father's papers," Mr. Potter explained, handing it to her. "I opened it only because I thought it might contain something that I should handle for you. I'm sure you realize that your father's sudden accident left many loose ends that I've had to take care of."

Arianna held the file for a moment. It was very much like all the others that she'd seen in her father's office at home and that were now on Mr. Potter's large desk. This one, however, had her name on the tab and a bright pink clip that marked it as a personal rather than a straight business file. Arianna hesitated a moment, suddenly not wanting to open it here with Mr. Potter's cold, analytical eyes watching her.

"I believe you should look at it now, Arianna," Mr. Potter added, his voice gentle but firm. "It is something we'll have to discuss."

Arianna smoothed down her chocolate linen suit and settled back into the chair before she opened the file. It contained only one small sheaf of papers, and the heading told her what Mr. Potter's tactful insistence had been about. She felt an all-too-familiar pang of disillusionment as she stared at the separation agreement, her eyes drawn to the names on it: Paul Roarke and Arianna Kane Roarke.

Hand shaking, she shifted the papers aside, seeking the second document that should have been beneath the first legal forms. "Where is the annulment?" she asked, looking up at Mr. Potter.

"Annulment?" He frowned at her.

Arianna stared at him, but she wasn't really seeing the middle-aged lawyer or his handsomely appointed office. Instead, her eyes were focused on the past and the man she'd thought was out of her life forever. The man her father had promised to banish. "There's just the separation agreement here," she explained. "Where are the rest of the papers?"

"I'm sorry, Arianna, but I've checked everything and there are no annulment or divorce papers. Our files show that neither my late partner nor I handled any such action. Once we had secured the legal separation for you, your father never mentioned the man again. Unless Mr. Roarke has taken some action that we weren't informed about, you are still legally man and wife and have been for five years."

"But Daddy said . . ." Arianna stopped to swallow the lump in her throat. "Mr. Potter, I've been engaged twice in the past four years and my father never said a word. Granted, we never set a wedding date either time, but surely if I wasn't legally free to marry, he would have said so. How could he not have told me?" She was ashamed to realize that the last words were almost a wail. The adding of old pain to new was more than she could bear.

Mr. Potter sighed and squirmed. "You know that I counted your father as a friend, Arianna," he began, waiting for her nod before he went on. "I was very fond of him, but surely you must know that your father had a character flaw, the same flaw that destroyed his financial empire at his death."

Arianna dropped her gaze to her lap. "You mean that since he didn't want to believe that I was still married, he decided that I wasn't?"

"He may have considered your marriage questionable, since you were married without his consent. Or he may have contacted Roarke and made some private arrangements with him. I do remember that your father was determined to have an annulment, but there was simply no legal basis to ask for one."

"So he simply dismissed the whole thing," Arianna finished for him.

Potter shrugged. "That was the year that the two of you spent in Europe. Perhaps by the time you returned, he'd simply forgotten."

Arianna forced a tight, bitter smile. She remembered that time well. "A grand tour," her father had called it, and in some ways it had been. He'd taken her everywhere, entertaining her lavishly, dressing her at the finest shops in France, showering her with gifts. She'd known that it was his way of making her feel like a whole person again after Paul's cruel betrayal, but no amount of fatherly love had been able to fill the hollow left by her broken heart.

"Whatever your father's reasons, Arianna, this is something that should be taken care of." Mr. Potter broke into her thoughts, his voice firm. "I realize that you've used the name Arianna Kane ever since your return from Europe, but legally, unless this Paul Roarke has ended the marriage, you are still Mrs. Paul Roarke."

"Would you find out for me?" Arianna asked, absorbing a fresh stab of pain at hearing herself called Mrs. Roarke. "I mean, whether Paul did get a divorce."

"I'll start making inquiries at once," Mr. Potter promised. "However, it may take some time, Arianna. The only address I have is the one given on the separation agreement, and that was five years ago."

Arianna got to her feet, returning the file to his desk. "When you find out where he is, I'd like to know."

Mr. Potter stood up too. "I'll also compile a comprehensive list of your father's holdings. And I'll make arrangements with the banks and other financial institutions involved, so that you can stay at the house until it's sold."

She nodded, the golden fall of her hair like honey flowing in the late-afternoon sunlight that entered the office through the tall windows. She moved numbly toward the door.

Never had she felt more abandoned, not even immediately after she'd received the news of her father's death. At least then she'd still been sure of his love and protection; but now the collapse of his empire had stripped away his protection. And somehow the news about Paul made her wonder about her father's love.

It wasn't that she cared about the money, she thought sadly as she left the familiar office. It was losing everything—her father, the land, the old mansion that had been her home for as long as she could remember. It was as though her whole life had been wiped out in the plane crash. And now to be reminded of Paul and all that had happened so long ago was a double blow.

Arianna got into the small light green coupé that had been her college-graduation gift from her father earlier in the month, but she didn't start the motor for a moment. Instead she took a minute to rest, slumped and weary. Out of the sight of prying eyes, she tried to absorb fully all that she'd just learned.

She closed her aching eyes, hating her father and loving him at the same time. Had she ever understood him? she wondered bitterly. He'd moved through her life like a comet, always blazing with life and laughter, bringing her gifts, calling her his princess, promising her whatever she wanted or needed. Yet in the end he'd left her more vulnerable in a somewhat frightening world than she'd ever imagined possible.

What should she do? she asked herself as she drove away from the lawyer's office. She had to go home and think. Mr. Potter had given her an amazing amount of information during the two hours of their meeting, and she had to deal with it in a positive way.

And Paul—what about him? Somehow she could think of no positive way to handle the feelings that churned through her at the mere mention of his name. Memories washed over her in waves, some so sweet and wonderful she ached with longing, others so bitter with pain she was more wounded by them than she had been by the day's news of her father's betrayal. She banished them with hard courage.

Once she was home, she went straight to the library, the room that had always been her father's. She sat at his desk and took out a sheet of paper. It was time to make lists, to decide what to keep and what to sell among the household furnishings. Her life of dependency was over; now she must take charge of herself.

Arianna worked for hours, not noticing the time slipping by until her head and back ached in protest.

She gave up and went to the second-floor suite of rooms that had been hers since her mother's death twenty years ago. Dropping on the bed, exhausted, she waited for tears, but she was beyond them.

Instead of reviewing today's pain, her mind traveled back in time to the days when she had first met Paul. How naive, how innocent she'd been then! The ease with which the memories came made it clear that they'd never been banished from her heart.

When she'd asked permission to spend a few weeks with her boarding-school roommate in Seattle the spring after her eighteenth birthday, her father had been surprisingly cooperative. "Stay with the Murrays as long as you like, honey," he told her over the phone. "Then you might bring Joy back to Denver with you for a while. I don't know how much time I'll be spending at the house while I'm working on this Latin-American deal, but Mrs. Cranston will be here to organize things for both of you."

Feeling depressed at the prospect of a lonely summer vacation in Colorado without her father, Arianna was pleased when Joy suggested a boat trip. They would cross the beautiful blue waters of Puget Sound, then go north to explore the many islands that dotted the channel between the mainland of Washington and British Columbia and the lovely coast of Vancouver Island.

The boat was the *Pellington Star,* an elderly fishing boat recently refurbished and converted to carry a half-dozen passengers in comfort for the tour. It was not, however, the boat that immediately claimed Arianna's attention; it was her captain.

"Welcome aboard, girls," he greeted them as Mr.

Murray escorted them up the gangplank to the deck. "I'm Paul Roarke, your captain."

He was tall, several inches over six feet, and his dark brown hair blew slightly in the breeze that came off the water. Green eyes studied them rather impersonally, first Joy, then Arianna. She felt herself blushing under his scrutiny and had to control an urge to make sure that her white slacks and brown-and-white T-shirt were smoothly in place.

Joy began asking questions about the boat as soon as her father went back to the dock, and Arianna felt a pang of envy as she watched her friend flirting with the handsome captain. Though she and Joy were the same age, Arianna was always less sure of herself. Years of spending her winters in boarding school and her summers under her father's protective eye had left her very inexperienced when it came to men. An attractive stranger like the captain left her tongue-tied with shyness.

"What do you think of him?" Joy asked as soon as they were alone in the small cabin they were to share for the five-day tour.

"He's very handsome," Arianna admitted as casually as she could. "And he seemed to like you."

"Oh, sure, he's mad for me," Joy answered with a grin that lit her dark blue eyes. "That's why he spent the entire time we were talking asking me about you."

"What?" Arianna put down the shorts set she'd just unpacked. "Don't tease me, Joy. I saw you batting those long eyelashes at him."

"Lot of good it did me." Joy sighed. "Sometimes I think blondes do have more fun."

"Considering I never had a date until you arranged one for me, I wouldn't say that was a very good conclusion for you to draw." Arianna smiled at her friend. She was grateful to Joy for helping her to meet and date boys, but sometimes she wasn't really comfortable socializing with people her own age. She'd spent too much of her life being her father's hostess and she was far more at home with older people. "What did you find out about the captain?" she asked, suddenly aware of the silence between them.

Joy's sparkling eyes narrowed speculatively. "Do I detect a little spark of interest in the good captain, Arianna?"

"Of course not," Arianna replied much too quickly. "He wouldn't be interested in me. I was just sort of curious."

"He's twenty-six, unmarried, and he owns the boat," Joy stated, turning her attention to her own unpacking. "He was raised on one of the islands north of here."

"My, my, you were efficient," Arianna teased. "Fifteen minutes of casual conversation and you have his whole history."

"It wasn't that hard," Joy observed. "He was so busy staring at you, he didn't know what he was talking about."

"He was probably hoping that I'd fall overboard so he could have you all to himself for the trip," Arianna told her. "I've seen you operate before, you know. You'll have him taking you to his island to meet his family. The rest of us will just have to be content looking at the scenery."

"Not as long as Barry and Tim are going to be along," Joy informed her with a wicked smile.

"Barry and Tim?" Arianna gasped. "What do you mean?"

Joy's blue eyes were dancing. "Now, just who do you think suggested this trip?" she asked.

Arianna shook her head. Barry and Tim were two of Joy's friends from Seattle. Barry was Joy's steady boyfriend and the four of them had been double-dating ever since she'd come to stay at the Murrays'. "Where were they when we came on board?" she asked at last, sensing that Joy wasn't pleased by her less-than-thrilled response to the news.

"They won't be joining us till tomorrow," Joy answered. "Barry couldn't get away today. Besides, Daddy might not have been too pleased to discover they were going to be on the boat with us. You know how stuffy he can be sometimes."

Arianna giggled. "If you think your father is stuffy, you should try living with mine. If he had his way, I wouldn't be allowed to see anyone without a chaperon till after my twenty-first birthday."

"Well, we won't have to worry about either father on this trip," Joy said smugly. "Just you and me, and Barry and Tim for entertainment."

"That should make the trip more interesting," Arianna agreed, aware that Joy expected her to be pleased. And she was, she told herself firmly, but there was also a touch of disappointment. Tim had been fun to be with on their dates, but there had been something so . . . so magnetic about Captain Roarke. She'd felt her pulse jump the moment his green eyes turned her way.

Could Joy have been telling the truth? she asked herself. But she immediately pushed the idea away. Captain Paul Roarke was definitely the type of man that was attracted to Joy. Arianna would just have to forget the effect he'd had on her and do her best to enjoy the boat tour and Tim's pleasant company.

The sound of the boat's motor suddenly broke the silence in the cabin and Arianna glanced longingly toward the small porthole. Masts were moving outside. "Shall we go up on deck?" she suggested.

"You go ahead," Joy said. "I'd better finish my unpacking. I've seen the harbor from a boat deck plenty of times."

"Oh, I can wait." Arianna tried not to let her disappointment show.

"Go on and see if I'm telling you the truth about our gorgeous captain," Joy teased. "Of course, he's probably pretty busy getting us out of the dock area, but he'll find a way to talk to you anyhow."

"Oh, Joy, I . . ." Arianna knew she was blushing and hated herself for it. She'd hoped to outgrow the childish habit, but somehow it still came over her when she least expected it.

"Are you going to be a coward all your life?" Joy demanded, her frown genuine. "You can't hide forever, Arianna. You'll be going to college in the fall, and this isn't the Dark Ages, no matter what your father thinks. Girls are allowed to be interested in guys, remember? It's all right to give them a chance to get to know you—if they want to."

Anger and resentment surged for a moment inside her; then Arianna's sense of humor asserted itself and she managed a reasonably genuine giggle. "All right, if you insist on matchmaking, I'll try to cooperate. But if it doesn't work, you'll just have to go back to flirting with him yourself."

"A fate I could learn to live with," Joy replied, giving Arianna a push toward the door of the cabin. "So get up on deck. I'll be along pretty soon for a progress report."

Arianna stepped out into the passageway with a chuckle, though she was sure that Captain Roarke would be far too busy with the boat to pay any attention to her. She headed for the deck anyway; this was her first cruise and she didn't want to miss anything.

Three steps along the passageway, however, the boat made a sudden lunge to the left, rocking so violently that she went crashing into the wood paneling. Strong hands caught her about the waist from behind, steadying her as the boat righted itself with another bounce.

"Careful there," a deep male voice said, and she looked up into green eyes. "We're going to need seat belts if my crew keeps that up."

She tried to respond to his teasing tone, but the words wouldn't form into sentences, not with his eyes boring into hers and his hands still touching the warm, sensitive flesh of her waist below the edge of her T-shirt. Slowly, gently, he eased her the rest of the way around to face him.

Electricity seemed to crackle in the narrow passageway, and her heart was beating so hard she was sure he must be able to see the force of its pounding at the base of her throat. He wanted to kiss her, her whirling thoughts told her. Pull away, she told herself, say something funny to divert him; but she couldn't. She could only stand there, held captive by the electricity between them, the wild attraction that was like nothing she'd ever felt before.

"Arianna, are you . . ." The sound of Joy's voice broke the spell, and Arianna pulled away from the captain guiltily, spinning to face her friend.

"Are you all right now, Miss Kane?" Captain Roarke asked.

"Yes, thank you, Captain," Arianna replied with a quick glance back at him. She kept her voice cold and flat, furious at him for so devastating her with a simple touch.

"Miss Murray." The captain nodded to Joy, then favored them both with a smile. "See you two on deck."

Joy said nothing till the captain had disappeared up the stairs that led to the deck; then she turned her blue eyes toward Arianna. "What was that I said about your being so shy and cowardly?" she asked, one dark eyebrow arched quizzically.

"Oh, Joy, I just stumbled when the boat rolled, and he was there. Nothing happened. He just saved me from a fall."

"I'd say his rescue technique requires some study," Joy teased. "Why don't you go up on deck and look into it?"

"Oh, I couldn't," Arianna protested. "I don't want to see him. What must he think of me, just standing there like a ninny and not saying anything? It's just that I was so surprised." She stopped, aware that she was making too much of the incident. Still, she felt certain that it hadn't been just a casual encounter.

Joy laughed. "I'll go with you and protect you from temptation," she said. "I've got everything unpacked."

Arianna followed Joy to the bustle on the deck. Much to her relief, Captain Roarke was nowhere to be seen. She moved to the rail, leaning on the well-polished wood and brass as she looked back at the dock they were leaving behind.

"When did you say Tim and Barry would be joining us?" she asked after a few minutes of silence had soothed the worst of her embarrassment.

"In Port Angeles tomorrow," Joy answered.

"Why didn't you tell me they were going to be on this trip?" Arianna asked.

"I was afraid you might not want to come if you knew," Joy admitted. "I mean, I know you're not too wild about Tim. But he is a nice guy, Arianna, and he'll be a good escort for five days." Joy paused; then her eyes sparkled wickedly. "Of course, I may spend the journey feeling sorry for poor Tim—he certainly can't compete with Captain Roarke."

"I'm sure he won't have to," Arianna snapped. "Just because I was a little clumsy in the passageway . . ." Their eyes met, and Arianna didn't go on. Memories of that electric moment swept over her, and she realized that she'd wanted him to kiss her. She'd wanted a perfect stranger to kiss her. It was madness.

"Enjoying the view?"

Chills raced down Arianna's spine, but she stayed very still, not turning to face Captain Roarke, who'd come up behind them. He put a sun-darkened hand on the rail beside hers, and she remembered how it had felt on her waist, the warm strength of his fingers. She forced herself to look away from his hand, to concentrate on the frothing blue water below.

"Where are we going?" Joy asked.

"The Morton Inn at Pine Harbor. We'll have dinner there, then anchor in the harbor for the night. Mrs. Morton is famous for her salmon dinners, so you're in for a treat."

"That's for sure," Joy agreed. "I've been to the inn several times with my family." She stopped, then added, "This will be Arianna's first visit, though. She's from Denver."

"I'm looking forward to it," Arianna managed, aware that they were both watching her. She was relieved when a shout from one of the crew members forced Captain Roarke to leave them.

Chapter Two

❦

Though Arianna professed weariness and lack of appetite that evening, Joy was insistent. "You are not going to miss tonight just because you're shy," she told Arianna. "We're going to dress up and we're going to have a good time. Now, what are you going to wear?"

Arianna produced a shimmering brown-and-gold-print dress that left her tanned shoulders bare except for thin gold straps and made the most of her slender but well-rounded figure. She was pleased when Joy swirled her honey-colored hair high in a curly knot. With the addition of dangling gold earrings, she knew she at least looked quite sophisticated.

The only other guests on the boat were an older couple, who joined Joy, Arianna, the captain, and a crew member named Mike Jeffers for dinner. The six of them sat together at a round oak table in the country-style inn. The kerosene lamps threw a gentle light over them and the conversation was easy and pleasant. Paul seemed to be concentrating on drawing everyone out and fostering a feeling of friendship that would make the close contact on the boat more pleasant. Arianna found it surprisingly easy to talk about herself as she told him about her college plans and her dreams of someday becoming an interior decorator.

By the time the final coffee was served, Arianna had managed to banish her remembered embarrassment. She smiled at Paul when the music started, and her heart lifted when he asked her to dance. She'd deliberately placed herself as far from him as she could when they sat down, so she was glad to have a chance to be closer, and she accepted with shy eagerness.

"Do you think I owe you an apology, Arianna?" Paul asked as they moved slowly around the floor, mingling with the other dancers.

"An apology?" Arianna looked up at him and felt the tension returning. She knew he was referring to the incident outside her cabin.

"You've been shy as a wild doe ever since this afternoon," he continued. "I'll admit to enjoying our little encounter, but I'd hate to have you avoiding me for the rest of the trip because of it."

Arianna felt the familiar warmth rising to her cheeks, but she fought the shyness that came with it. "Oh, I think we can safely forget this afternoon," she told him in her best imitation of Joy's flirtatious style. "It was just one of those moments."

She was proud of her casualness, though she hadn't quite been able to bring herself to meet his eyes, fearing that he would perceive her response to him. His arms tightened suddenly, forcing her close to him. Startled, she looked up at him and the same wild tide of excitement pulsed through her. The soft lights seemed to dim around them and she was vaguely conscious that they were no longer moving in time to the music.

His lips descended toward hers, but this time there was no interruption from Joy. Her eyes closed and the magic of the kiss wrapped itself around her, making her cold and warm at the same time. She was conscious of the hard length of his body against her; the tangy scent of his after-shave filled her nostrils, making her dizzy.

His embrace loosened slightly as he freed her lips, but instead of letting her go, he led her through the French doors out to the wood-railed porch that surrounded the inn on three sides. The moon was rising over the pines, its nearly full contours reflected like liquid silver in the restless waters of the sound.

"I don't think we're going to be able to forget it, Arianna," he said softly, holding her lightly with one arm while he followed the line of her jaw with a finger. He traced the shape of her full lips with that same finger, the caress adding impact to his earlier kiss. "It's not just a moment for us. I knew that the second I saw you coming aboard. I recognized you from my dreams, Arianna Kane. I've waited all my life for you."

"But you don't even—" His lips stopped her protests, and as the stars reeled wildly overhead, her objections faded from her mind. It was all the magical dreams she'd treasured through her lonely years at boarding school. Her heart swelled with the first delight of love, and she clung to him, willing to believe in love at first sight.

"You will be mine, Arianna," he whispered. His words were strangely solemn and she felt them echo like a shiver down her spine as his lips moved sensuously down the line of her neck. When he lifted his head, she looked up at him, thrilled. His eyes, dark in the moonlight, were intense as they met hers. The sensation of meeting his gaze unnerved her, and she was glad when they rejoined the dancers inside.

But long before she had recovered from the encounter, Paul asked, "Ready for a last dance, Arianna?"

"Do we have to leave so early?" Joy pouted, her reluctance telling Arianna that she'd enjoyed Mike Jeffers' company.

"Mrs. Morton closes in half an hour," Paul answered, his fingers caressing Arianna's back in a slow, sensuous rhythm. "Besides, we'll be sailing early tomorrow."

Arianna went into his arms happily, not eager to think about tomorrow, wanting only to savor this last dance with Paul.

"You're the quiet one," he observed, tucking her head gently against him, his height and broad shoulders making her feel delicate and fragile.

"I guess I never learned how to make small talk." She lifted her head to look up at him, unaware of the way the soft light made deep pools of her wide, dark eyes and caressed the golden perfection of her skin and hair.

"I'm glad you didn't," Paul whispered, bending down to kiss the tip of her nose. "Most of the girls on the cruises are like Joy, out for a casual flirtation. But you're not a casual girl, sweet Arianna, that much I've learned tonight, just listening to you talk about things."

She lifted her hand from his shoulder to touch the slight curve of his sideburn, feeling the softness of his hair. "And you?" she asked. "Are you casual or serious?"

His chuckle was low and sensual and the fire in his

eyes caressed her face. "I've been casual for a long time, little girl, but perhaps now . . . Well, we'll have to see about that, won't we? You'll be staying with Joy for a while after the tour, so we can get to know each other very well."

His arm tightened and she surrendered to the rhythm of the music, letting her cheek settle against the rough fabric of his forest-green jacket. She was very conscious of his body, the heat that she could feel through the material of her dress, the steady pounding of his heart.

All too soon the music ended. Paul held her close in the quiet. "How about a walk along the beach before we go back to the *Star*?" he suggested.

"I'd love to," Arianna agreed.

The night breeze was cool and slightly damp when they stepped outside. The Websters, Mike, and Joy were already well out on the long dock, and the breeze brought the distant sound of Joy's giggle when they stopped at the edge of the shore.

"Give me your shoes," Paul said as they left the stepping-stone path that connected the inn and the dock. "You don't want to ruin them in the sand."

Arianna slipped off her sandals and handed the wisps of leather to Paul. They looked strange dangling from the fingers of his strong brown hands, and being barefoot beside him made her feel very small and vulnerable. She was suddenly aware of a tension in the air that hadn't been there before.

"It's lovely here," she murmured, trying to bridge the silence. "This is a nice beach."

"Are you a connoisseur of beaches?"

"Well, I spent the Christmas holidays in the Bahamas with my father last year and in Hawaii the year before,"

Arianna replied. "We spent a lot of time on the beach, but of course, the sand was different there. I mean, different places have different sand, and ..." She stopped, aware that she was making no sense. She was simply stumbling over words in an attempt to impress him with her sophistication.

"So, you're quite well-traveled." His tone held an undercurrent of amusement that rankled. "From what you said earlier, I thought you spent most of your time at school."

Arianna realized painfully just how foolish her words must sound to a man of the world like Paul Roarke. "My father's business involves a great deal of traveling," she responded quietly. "Whenever I'm free, he takes me with him."

Paul stopped and turned her to face him, his fingers lightly lifting her chin. "I'm not trying to embarrass you, Arianna," he told her, his shadowed features stern. "I only want to know you—you, not your laughing friend Joy or some sophisticated person you've imagined. I want to know what goes on behind those big brown eyes. I have a feeling it's much more interesting than fast banter or flirting."

She looked up into his eyes, feeling again the magic that vibrated between them even when his touch was so light. Was it because he was so handsome? she asked herself, and knew that it was not. His features were good, but not glamorous. It was the fire in his eyes that caught at her, that and the strange gentleness of his lips, which seemed at times out of place on his stern face.

There was a soft sound as he dropped her shoes to the cool sand, and his hands were warm on her arms as he held her away from him, looking at her. His eyes moved over her slowly, from her half-buried, naked toes up to the gold belt that secured her dress, then hesitated for a moment at the full swell of her breasts before they at last met her gaze. He released her arms and lifted his hands to pull the pins from her hair, allowing it to fall like a warm curtain over her neck and shoulders.

He caressed her wavy curls; then his fingers tangled in the softness of her hair and his arm went around her waist, pulling her close, so close she could feel the sharpness of his jacket buttons against her body. His head bent and he claimed her lips, caressing them tenderly with his own until they parted and allowed him the sweetness of her mouth.

Though she had kissed often enough since Joy had taken over her social life, nothing had prepared her for the wild surge of excitement that spread from her lips to her entire body. She clung to Paul, caressing the spiky hair on the back of his neck, feeling the firm ridges of muscle on his back as his embrace tightened so that she could hardly breathe.

When, after a lifetime of sensations, his arms loosened again and his lips lifted, she continued to cling to him, unwilling to step away from the blazing fire that had ignited between them. His hands moved on her back, caressing her shoulder blades, moving lower to rub the narrowing flesh of her waist, then tracing gently up her spine to the top of her dress. He moved away from her slightly, his hand coming around to follow the gold-trimmed top of the dress, tracing a shivering line across the tops of her breasts, then moving to her neck and throat as though he were seeing her not with his eyes, but with the tips of his fingers. He sighed and she could feel something very like a shudder passing through his body.

"You are definitely not a casual girl, Arianna Kane," he whispered. "And it is time that we went back to the boat."

He bent to retrieve her shoes, and the cold night air washed over her too-warm body, making her shiver as much with longing as with the cold. Paul seemed to sense her feelings, for he slipped off his jacket and set it lightly on her shoulders, his hands gentle. She snuggled into it, her senses reeling with the mingled joy of his scent and the warm feeling of his body that still lingered in the jacket's folds.

"You'll be cold," she protested.

"Not tonight," he answered, putting an arm around her shoulders as they moved through the sand, slipping and sliding so that their sides touched often and intimately. "Not while you're beside me, Arianna."

She wanted to tell him that she felt the same way, but words wouldn't come. She had no experience with expressing her emotions, and the very intensity of her feelings bound her tongue. She could only look up at him, delighting in the way he smiled at her.

At the dock, they stopped and he knelt in the sand to slip first one sandal, then the other on her feet. His fingers first moved slowly to brush away the sand, caressing it off her skin with a movement so sensuous she longed to drop to the sand beside him. There was an intimacy about the moment that kept them silent, and she was almost relieved when he only took her hand for the walk out to the boat. For the first time she was afraid, not of Paul, but of what she was feeling.

"We're going to have a wonderful cruise, little one," he whispered when they reached her cabin door. "I'll show you my world, and I think you'll love it as much as I do."

"I know I will," Arianna agreed.

"Good night, love," he said, bending to kiss her so lightly that she hardly felt his lips. He was gone before she could stop him, before she could answer his kiss with the blazing longing that filled her. She stood looking after him for several minutes before she finally opened the cabin door and floated in.

"Well, well, well," Joy said from the vanity where she'd been putting a few pins in her mop of dark curls, "it's about time you got home. What have you been up to, as if I didn't know."

Arianna was too happy to care about Joy's embarrassing tone. "We walked in the sand," she answered.

"Somehow I don't see cold, damp sand making your eyes glow like that. Tell me, was I right about the good captain?"

"He's wonderful," Arianna breathed, sitting down on her narrow bed, too enraptured even to remove her dress.

"Poor Tim," Joy murmured. "It's too bad it's too late to warn him."

"Tim." Arianna said the name without recognition, lost in the magic of her memory of the kiss on the beach.

Joy sighed, her eyes compassionate. "Get undressed, Arianna," she instructed.

Arianna smiled at her for several minutes, then drifted to her feet and began to obey. She was dimly conscious that Joy was continuing to talk to her, but she was too happy to listen. He had called her "love"; he'd kissed her and said he wanted to know her better. She remembered the way he'd told her that she would be his, and she shivered, unsettled by the passions his kiss had unleashed, the desires that she was just learning she possessed.

Though she'd thought she was too excited to sleep, she was lost in dreams of love the moment her head touched the pillow. In all of them, the man who held, kissed and caressed her was Paul Roarke. She woke with a smile and a sigh, wishing that the dreams could last forever, yet anxious for the day to begin.

"I thought you were going to sleep all day," Joy told her. "We've been under way for nearly an hour."

Arianna scrambled out of bed. "Why didn't you wake me?" she asked, hurrying to wash and pull on navy shorts and a red-white-and-navy blouse.

"Every time I thought about it, you'd just sigh and smile in your sleep. You seemed to be having such wonderful dreams, I couldn't bring myself to disturb you. I am, however, starving to death, so let's go eat before the food is all gone."

Arianna divided her hair into two golden ponytails, which she tied with red ribbons. "I look twelve," she moaned in despair.

"You can do something with your hair later," Joy informed her unsympathetically. "After breakfast."

Since she was also hungry, Arianna accepted the urging and followed her friend along the passage to the common room, which served as dining room and lounge for the passengers and crew of the boat. She was both relieved and disappointed to find that the room was empty of everything but breakfast.

"Looks like everyone else has eaten," Joy observed, heading across to the recessed serving table where several warming pans simmered promisingly. "Let's just hope they left something. Being on the water always makes me ravenous." She lifted the lids on the pans. "Ah, we're in luck."

They filled their plates with eggs, sausage, French toast, and sweet rolls, then carried them to the table before picking up fresh juice and coffee. Joy ate in silence for several minutes, then fixed Arianna with a stern eye. "So what about last night?" she asked. "I mean, was it a wonderful fling or is he going to want to shove Tim overboard?"

Arianna smiled. "It was the most wonderful and exciting evening of my life. But I just don't know what to tell him about Tim. How do I explain?"

"You didn't tell him last night?" Joy looked surprised. "I thought you told him on the beach. You were out there long enough."

"Actually, I didn't think about it," Arianna admitted, memories of the passionate abandon of their kiss overwhelming her anew.

Joy giggled. "I'm sorry, Arianna," she said. "I just never dreamed when I invited them to join us that you'd be finding someone like Paul Roarke waiting on board for you."

"Just so it doesn't ruin everything," Arianna muttered. "Tim's nice, but Paul . . ."

"You've really got it bad for him," Joy observed, a tiny frown touching her forehead. "Just be careful, will you? Take it slow, Arianna. A man like Paul Roarke can sweep you off your feet and hurt you badly doing it."

Arianna was about to protest, but she ruefully recognized that Joy had the one thing she lacked—experience. She swallowed her retort, fearing Joy might be right.

"Don't look so stricken," Joy told her. "I'm not saying that you shouldn't have an utterly terrific time with Captain Paul. I just think you should remember that this is only a five-day tour and you don't know what will happen when it's over."

"He told me last night that he wanted to see me after the tour," Arianna informed her quickly.

"Just be careful," Joy repeated. "And that's my last word on the subject."

"I promise," Arianna agreed, though she had a strange feeling that it was already too late for any warning.

They ate in silence for several minutes, Joy going back to refill her plate while Arianna toyed with a second piece of French toast, her thoughts still on the night before. Was it just a game with Paul? she asked herself uncertainly. Was it possible that he did this with his passengers whenever there was one that attracted his eye? She had a horrible feeling that it could be true. Her appetite faded further as she asked herself what a suave, sophisticated man like Paul Roarke could find to interest him in a girl like her. Never had she felt younger or less able to cope with the day ahead.

"So, do you want to go up on deck and watch as we land at Port Angeles?" Joy asked, finishing her coffee with a satisfied sigh.

"When will we be landing?" Arianna asked, not looking forward to Barry's and Tim's arrival, since she still didn't know what she was going to say or do about it.

Joy shrugged. "Before noon."

"I think I'd better go back to the cabin and do something with my hair," Arianna murmured, tugging at one of the ponytails.

"I think you should leave it just that way," Joy argued. "It looks darling, plus it's practical on deck, where there's always wind and spray. If you fix it now, it'll be all messed up before dinner anyway."

"Where do we have dinner?" Arianna asked, sensing that her friend had something specific in mind.

"Somewhere special in Victoria, I imagine," Joy answered. "This cruise supplies breakfast and lunch only. We anchor somewhere and go ashore for each evening meal."

"Well, then, I guess I might as well go up on deck," Arianna acknowledged, aware that her heartbeat quickened at the very thought. Paul Roarke would, undoubtedly, be somewhere on the deck of the boat, and in spite of her morning doubts, she wanted very much to see him.

Chapter Three

❧

"Hey, I think we must be coming into the harbor already," Joy said as the rhythm of the motor changed and the boat shifted direction.

"Joy, what should I do?" Arianna gasped, suddenly filled with a strong desire to duck into the cabin and stay there.

"You're going to go up on deck with me and welcome Barry and Tim aboard," Joy answered. "Then, after they get settled, we'll decide what to do."

Arianna glared at her. "Thanks a lot."

Joy shrugged. "So we'll think of something. Now, come on."

When they stepped out into the sunlight on deck, Arianna was shocked to see how close they were to the dock. Barry and Tim were clearly in view, waving eagerly. She looked around for Paul, wanting to see him, to read in his eyes what last night had meant to him. He was, however, nowhere in sight.

The boat moved smoothly into place alongside the dock. Mike Jeffers and another crewman came forward to unload several items from the small cargo area on the deck while Barry and Tim came up the gangplank, looking pleased and happy. Joy ran forward to welcome Barry with a kiss, but Arianna held back, still wondering where Paul might be.

Tim slowed and she could see the indecision in his gray eyes as he ran a hand through his sandy hair. Guilt swept over her. It wasn't his fault after all, she reminded herself. He probably thought that she had wanted him to come along—as she might have, if it hadn't been for Paul. She forced a welcoming smile.

"Welcome aboard!" she said with a smile. "You—"

Tim stepped forward and pulled her into his arms, bending his head to kiss her just as Barry had kissed Joy. Arianna tensed, her hands lifting to push him away.

"Tim, please," she protested, feeling strangely trapped.

"Arianna, don't be shy, now," Tim teased. "After all, you did invite me on this trip so we'd have a chance to get to know each other better." His tone made it clear that his idea of knowing her better had little to do with conversation.

Before Arianna could reply, another hand landed on her shoulder and Tim backed away, releasing his hold on her at once.

"Welcome aboard, gentlemen," Paul said, his tone curiously cool. "I was just coming to introduce you to the rest of the passengers, but I see you've already met. I'm Paul Roarke, your captain."

Arianna turned to look at Paul, then wished she hadn't, for there was nothing she recognized in his face. His green eyes might well have been ice and there was no tenderness in the expression of his mouth.

An awkward silence spread, and Arianna groped for
something to say, something that would ... Would
what? she asked herself bitterly. Tell Paul that she
hadn't invited Tim? That would solve nothing, since
Tim was here and obviously eager for the trip. Why
hadn't she told Paul everything last night?

"Well, shall we show you where your cabin is?" Joy
asked, breaking the silence. "You'll want to get unpacked before we cast off for Victoria."

Paul's smile didn't touch his eyes. "You've been as-
signed cabin four," he told them. "Right across the
passageway from your friends."

Joy took Barry's arm and moved toward the compan-
ionway that led down to the cabins, and Tim took
Arianna's arm, tugging her after them. Arianna looked
back over her shoulder to say something to Paul, but
he'd already moved down the gangplank to talk to
several people on the dock.

Arianna stumbled down the steps, practically shaking
with frustration. He hated her! Paul believed that she'd
just been having fun last night, that she was the kind of
girl who would throw herself at one man while she was
waiting for another to arrive. If only she could go back
and do the evening over.

Tim interrupted her thoughts when they reached the
passageway. "Don't worry, Arianna. We're going to have
fun on this tour, just watch. Barry and I have been
most of the places we're going, so we've got all kinds of
things planned."

"Why don't you two get unpacked and we'll meet you
up on deck," Arianna suggested, her longing to escape
tinged with a need to see Paul, to steal a moment to try
to explain.

"Who needs to unpack?" Barry asked, dropping his small suitcase on his bed. "We didn't come on this trip to hang around inside. I'm just sorry we couldn't get on with you last night. Did you have a good time at the Morton Inn?"

"Absolutely terrific," Arianna answered before Joy could speak. "It was a perfect place and the food and music were just wonderful." She stopped, realizing they were all looking at her.

Joy looked pained, swallowed hard, then took a deep breath. However, before she could speak, Barry caught her in his arms and kissed her. "I don't know whether you had that much fun last night or not," he said with mock severity, "but from now on, we will, I promise."

Joy shot Arianna a hopeless glance, then led the way back to the deck. Arianna looked around, hoping to see Paul, but he seemed to have vanished. In a moment Mike was shouting orders and the lines were cast off so that the boat chugged out of the harbor.

She stayed at the rail, staring back at the lovely scene, but seeing nothing beyond the coldness in Paul's eyes. He wouldn't speak to her again, she told herself bitterly. They would spend the next four days avoiding each other on the boat, and then she'd be back in Seattle and she'd never see him again. The thought was so painful she had to swallow a sob.

"Hey, there. Earth to Arianna . . . come in, please." Tim's tone was light, but there was something cold in his eyes when she turned to look at him.

"I'm sorry, Tim," she said. "What did you say?"

"I asked you if you knew what we were supposed to do once we reach Victoria. What's wrong, Arianna? Aren't you feeling well?"

"We were out late last night and I'm not fully awake yet," Arianna replied, trying to smile in apology. "Anyway, I don't know if there's anything planned for Victoria. I never asked." She turned back to the receding shoreline to avoid meeting his eyes again.

"Well, I have plans," Tim told her. "I want to take you to Butchart Gardens to watch the sunset in the most romantic setting you can imagine."

"We'll have to talk to Barry and Joy," Arianna said quickly. "And I'm not sure what Paul . . . I mean Captain Roarke has planned."

"Did I hear my name mentioned?" Paul's voice made her pulses race even as she felt a twinge of panic at his approach.

"We were wondering about the arrangements in Victoria." Tim spoke before she could do more than turn to face Paul.

Paul's smile was tight and his eyes were blazing with an emotion she preferred not to name. "I've made all the necessary arrangements," he answered. "We'll be met at the dock by a limousine for a tour of the city, then we'll drive out to Butchart Gardens and spend as long as you like there, coming back to a special seafood restaurant for dinner before returning to the *Star*. How does that sound?"

Arianna was aware of a stiff agreement from Tim and murmurs of approval from the others, but she remained silent herself, her gaze imprisoned by Paul's flashing emerald eyes. She could feel the anger in his glare, but there was something else mixed with it. His gaze was a challenge, a warning that she would soon have to face him with an explanation.

"I'm sure you'll enjoy it all," Paul continued, his eyes

still holding hers hypnotically, as though he spoke the words for her alone. "Victoria is one of the loveliest cities in the world."

For a final moment he continued to meet her gaze; then he turned away, leaving her feeling limp and somewhat violated. She turned once more to the rail, her eyes seeking relief in the froth that the boat tore from the blue waters.

"Who does he think he is?" Tim asked, his tone angry. "He acts like he owns us. What if we don't want to do what he said?"

Joy giggled. "He's the captain and this is his tour," she replied. "I'm sure he just arranged what he thought would be a pleasant outing for all of us. It's what we would do anyway, isn't it, Barry?" She looked up at the tall, mahogany-haired young man beside her.

Barry's grin was warm, as always. "He's just saving us the trouble of trying to find a car to rent and maybe missing most of the city sights," he agreed with Joy, something he always seemed to do, no matter what the sparkling brunette suggested.

"If you'd rather not go with the group," Arianna began, but Tim looked at her strangely.

"Oh, no, I guess it'll be okay," he replied in a somewhat embarrassed tone. He didn't continue, and Arianna didn't press him to. She knew well enough what he resented and she understood that he had a right to those feelings, since she hadn't been honest with him.

The balance of the morning was spent cruising along the coast for sightseeing in the Strait of Juan de Fuca, which gave access to the Pacific Ocean. Paul ordered a retracing of their course before actually reaching the open sea, and they returned to the more sheltered waters of the Inside Passage, heading for Victoria.

Though she saw Paul only in passing, Arianna was aware that he was watching her and that made her doubly conscious of each time Tim touched her hand or arm. She found herself unable to respond to his conversation in anything beyond monosyllables. She was glad when Joy suggested that they should go to their cabin to change before lunch.

Once in the privacy of the cabin, Arianna sank down on her bunk in despair. "What am I going to do, Joy?" she asked.

Joy looked guilty. "Maybe I could tell Barry today and let him explain it to Tim," she suggested. "It might be easier for him, hearing it that way."

"I just feel so awful," Arianna wailed. "But there's nothing I can do. I just can't get my mind off Paul."

Joy said nothing, her blue eyes narrowed. "You might be better off with Tim," she observed at last. "At least you know that he'll be around next fall when you go to college."

Arianna said nothing. She understood her friend's warning and even shared her doubts, but it was simply beyond her control. When Paul Roarke came anywhere near her, everyone else just faded into the background. Scary or not, it was too exciting for her to ignore.

"Do you want me to explain it all to Barry?" Joy asked.

Arianna nodded silently.

"Tim is going to be angry," Joy warned.

"I'll apologize to him," Arianna promised. "I just can't tell him what happened. I'd be too embarrassed."

"So what are you going to wear?" Joy asked, changing the subject with a firm determination that told Arianna she really didn't want to discuss it further.

Arianna sighed and forced herself to get to her feet and start looking at the clothes hanging in the small closet. "I guess this," she said, taking out a full-skirted tangerine sundress and jacket. "What do you think?"

"Other than a feeling of abject jealousy, I like it." Joy's tone was light. "I think I'll wear my lavender. We'll look like flowers."

"I don't suppose we'll be noticed in the Butchart Gardens," Arianna teased. "I hear the floral competition there is pretty strong."

Joy laughed. "That's the ticket," she counseled, her eyes serious. "Just have fun today and try not to worry about anything. Maybe it will all work out."

Arianna really didn't share her optimism, but she withheld any comment, simply slipping into the well-fitted dress before setting to work on her hair, which was escaping from the red ribbons she'd tied it with. It seemed desperately important that she look her best today. It took a little extra work, but finally her hair surrendered to flower-encrusted combs and fell in smooth waves on one side, while it was swept sleekly back on the other.

Victoria proved to be more beautiful than she'd imagined. The limousine took them first to a spot where they all climbed aboard one of the awning-sheltered, horse-drawn sightseeing wagons that plied the charming streets of the city. It moved slowly through the area that was sweet with the scents of the flowers that bloomed in gaily colored profusion in the baskets that hung from the streetlights.

Arianna stared in awe at the ivy-draped dowager that

was the elegant Empress Hotel, then turned her attention to the Parliament Buildings and other sights that Paul was pointing out. It was a city of variety and grace, much of which they continued to discover once they returned to the comfort of the limousine.

Though she tried to take Joy's advice, Arianna found herself unable to fully concentrate on the sights. Paul was playing the perfect host, charming Mrs. Webster as well as Joy. But every time he looked her way or managed to somehow have the seat beside her, neither he nor Arianna spoke.

Finally Paul touched the driver's arm. "I think it's time we went to the gardens," he said. "I want everyone to have all the time they need to enjoy them, and we'll be dining at eight."

The driver's answer was in soft French, which Paul seemed to understand. They conferred for several moments; then the limousine began picking up speed as they left the crowded city streets behind.

The scent of roses reached out to them the moment they left the air-conditioned interior of the limousine. Arianna stopped and sniffed, then laughed. "When they say gardens, they aren't fooling, are they?"

"Wait till you see them," Joy answered. "It's not like anything you've ever seen before."

"This way, folks," Paul said as he led them along the path from the parking area to the main gate.

The gardens were separate, and each was a living work of art. Profusely blooming rosebushes grew in patterns that set out a theme and executed it with precision. There were fountains and pools to complete the compositions, and each was more beautiful than the last.

They had just started down into the fourth display when a call came from behind them. Paul turned back. The driver from the limousine called something in rapid French, the only understandable words of which were "Tim Cooper."

"It seems there's a message for you at the entrance gate," Paul told Tim. "It must be something urgent."

Tim frowned. "Who could know that I'm here?" The question was addressed to no one in particular.

Paul's smile was easy. "If they contacted the boat, Mike would have told them that you were here. He knows our itinerary."

"I guess I'd better go see what it's all about," Tim said reluctantly.

Tim left with the driver and Paul quickly sent the rest of the group on to the next garden before he half-dragged Arianna off the path and into a small bower formed by carefully trimmed bushes. "Now," he said, "suppose you tell me what the hell is going on with you, Arianna."

Arianna met his gaze firmly. "Joy invited Barry and Tim on the trip, Paul," she began. "She didn't even tell me about it till after we left Seattle. I've been double-dating with Tim while I visited Joy." She stopped, unsure how to explain her feelings.

"Why didn't you tell me yesterday?" Paul asked.

She tried to think of an acceptable excuse, then decided to simply tell the truth. "I forgot."

For a moment Paul's stern eyes searched hers with a scrutiny that seemed to probe beneath the surface to the very depth of her pounding heart; then suddenly he was laughing. Arianna jerked away from his hand,

which was still on her arm. "It's not funny," she growled.
"I feel just awful."

Paul's laughter stopped as suddenly as it had begun,
and before she could move, his arms were around her
and she was crushed to him. He bent to her, his lips
seeking hers, claiming them with authority. Her lips
opened and her tongue met his in a touching, caressing,
tantilizing dance of delight. It seemed an eternity till
his lips freed hers, and she made no move to pull away.
She wanted only his embrace, the wonder of his touch.

"Does he make you feel this way?" Paul asked softly.

"No one has ever made me feel this way," she
answered, beyond hiding her feelings.

"He means nothing to you?"

She shook her head. "He's just Barry's best friend."

"Then I'm glad I arranged these few minutes alone
with you." Paul's eyes caressed her intimately, though
his hands were still on her shoulders. "I have no inten-
tion of sharing you with anyone, my Arianna. Now that
I've found you . . ." His lips finished the sentence far
more explicitly than words ever could.

"What about Tim?" Arianna asked when her whirling
thoughts allowed her to think clearly again.

"Don't give him another thought, little one," Paul
advised. "Just enjoy the roses."

They moved back to the display area, and Tim joined
them, his face flushed with anger. "It wasn't a call for
me at all," he complained. "That fool driver got the
name wrong."

"His English is pretty limited," Paul agreed blandly.
"Well, shall we hurry along and catch up with the
others?"

They continued their stroll through the gardens, but

Arianna found it difficult to concentrate on the flowers as she pondered Paul's words. It was a relief when Paul announced that they had to return to the limousine if they were to make their dinner reservations on time.

The restaurant proved to be a surprise. It was old, charmingly restored, and located almost on the water's edge. Wide glass windows gave a panoramic view of trees, water, and a rocky beach that seemed strangely wild and untouched by the people that laughed and talked and ate around them. The food was excellent, but Arianna's taste was dulled by the myriad of emotions that rippled through her every time her eyes met Paul's.

Darkness had hidden the land before they returned to the *Pellington Star*. Arianna was longing for a few moments alone with Joy to tell her what had happened and to ask her if she had talked to Barry for her. Barry, however, had other ideas. He quickly suggested to Joy that they take a stroll around the deck "to admire the moonlight."

"What do you say we join them, Arianna?" Tim asked immediately, his hand damp on her arm.

"Thanks, but not tonight," Arianna said. "I've developed the most awful headache. I think it must have been the roses, maybe a little allergy."

"Would you like me to see you to your cabin, Arianna?" Paul suggested.

"I think I can handle that, Captain," Tim asserted angrily.

"Thank you both," Arianna said, "but I think I can find it on my own. Good night, and thank you for a lovely day."

She ran down the steps to the quiet passageway and

let herself into the cabin with a sigh of relief. Coward
or not, she couldn't face a romantic moment with Tim,
knowing that Paul would be looking on from the bridge,
and she was simply too tired to explain everything to
Tim tonight. What was happening between her and
Paul was still too new and confusing to explain to
anyone else.

Sleep offered a refuge, and she accepted it eagerly,
succeeding so well she didn't even hear Joy's return
from the deck. A change in the motion of the boat
roused her the next morning, and she sat up yawning,
her smile left over from the happy dreams she'd been
having.

But before long memories of yesterday's problems
came to haunt her and she looked over at Joy's sleeping
form, wondering if she'd told Barry and if he, in turn,
had told Tim. She tried to return to sleep, but she was
far too wide-awake, and after a few more minutes of
twisting and twitching in her bunk, she got up and
dressed in clean shorts and a halter top. Brushing her
hair back casually, she headed for the common room,
determined to tell Tim herself if no one else had.

The common room was empty when she entered, but
she'd barely started filling her plate when Barry came
in looking sleepy-eyed and grumpy. His good-morning
was so cold that for a moment Arianna was too startled
to speak. However, once she was seated at the table and
had a sip of coffee, she plunged in.

"Will Tim be along soon?" she asked.

"Not bloody likely," Barry snapped.

"What do you mean?"

"He left at Victoria. He's probably waiting for the
ferry back to Seattle right now."

"What?" Arianna just blinked at him.

"The captain offered him a full refund right after he gave him your little bombshell," Barry went on, his expression not softening at all.

"What are you talking about?"

"Why didn't you have the decency to tell Tim that you and Captain Roarke are going to be married?" Barry asked. "I mean, I know you didn't set this up, but you could have done that much, couldn't you?"

Arianna just stared at him, too shocked to answer.

Chapter Four

૨૭

They were still sitting in silence when Joy came in, looking sleepy and hungry. But her attention was distracted from the food when she stopped at the table and looked from one to the other.

"I guess Arianna told you about the captain," she observed, feigning casualness.

"She didn't have to," Barry answered, some of his grumpiness fading as he looked up at her. He told Joy the same thing he'd just told Arianna.

Joy's eyes widened. "When did all that take place?" she demanded, her gaze meeting Arianna's.

"It didn't," Arianna muttered, still in a state of shock. "I mean . . . I told Paul yesterday that I . . . that having Tim on board was your idea, Joy, but that was all."

Though she was dimly conscious that Joy and Barry continued to talk, she heard nothing of their conversation. Her mind whirled around the words Barry had said. Two warring emotions rose in response: anger at Paul's presumptuousness and a resolve-weakening desire to surrender to the idea.

As she tried to think, she ate, not tasting anything, but chewing and swallowing from reflex. Her plate was almost empty when Paul came into the common room, a slightly triumphant smile on his face.

"Well, how is everyone feeling this morning?" he asked.

Silence echoed through the room as Barry glared and Joy kept her eyes on her plate. Arianna tried to pretend that she wasn't in the room, but she could feel his eyes like a burning torch on her face, and she had to look up.

"We'll be stopping at Nanaimo after lunch," Paul continued, his smile not touching his eyes as they met hers with a mixture of doubt and challenge. "There are several things to see there. Then, in the late afternoon we'll sail to a nearby island for dinner."

"We aren't having dinner at Nanaimo?" Barry asked, sounding surprised. "I thought that was on the itinerary."

"There's been a change of plans." Paul's eyes never left Arianna's. "I think you'll enjoy this island more than the restaurant in Nanaimo."

Barry got up abruptly. "I'll be on deck," he growled at Joy, and left without looking back.

Joy stayed where she was for a moment, then calmly placed her remaining bacon and eggs between two slices of toast and left, munching contentedly. The common room then seemed to shrink around Arianna and the captain, the air crackling with tension.

Paul sighed, then went to get a cup of coffee before he sank down across from her. "Are you very angry with me, Arianna?" he asked quietly.

The words were so gentle they had a disarming effect. She licked her dry lips, seeking words that would clarify her feelings and force him to explain why he'd told Tim such a monstrous lie. "You lied to Tim," she managed at last.

"No, I didn't." His expression was calm, unchanged.

Anger swept away her other feelings for a moment. "You told him that we were going to be married."

His smile was lazy, mocking. "He didn't want to leave you," he told her. "I had to tell him that to make him accept the fact that you are mine."

"Yours?" The words sent chills through her. "What do you think I am?" she demanded. "I'm not a piece of property to be claimed or bargained over!"

"Or won?" His lips tightened and the green eyes gleamed with a new light that made her throat dry and her breath quicken.

Arianna had the feeling that she was teetering on the edge of something, but she had no idea how to pull back to safety. The only hands held out to her were Paul's, and to touch him was an even greater danger.

"Don't be frightened, Arianna," he said, his tone changing again. "I won't hurt you. Just let me guide you, love you as I do, that's all I ask. You told me that you didn't want Tim around, so I saw to it that he left. Just leave it at that. We have time now, all the time we'll need."

"Paul." The male voice made them both jump nervously, for they'd been so intent on each other they hadn't heard Mike approaching. "I don't mean to interrupt, but there's a radio call."

Paul got to his feet at once, his face assuming the assured expression of the ship's captain. "Of course, Mike," he said. "We'll talk more later, Arianna." His fingers brushed her cheek as he came around the table and passed her chair.

Arianna stayed where she was, her cheek feeling burned, her pulses slowing only after several moments. What had he meant? Time for what? Had the words about marriage simply been a convenient lie, or was he serious? He'd said that he loved her, but was it the kind of love that meant marriage, or was it only wild desire that blazed between them?

There were no answers in the empty room, and after a while she could bear it no longer and went up on deck to join Barry and Joy and the Websters. The coast that they were following was beautiful enough to distract her from her personal problems, at least for the moment.

In spite of her doubts, the day passed easily. Nanaimo proved to be a charming town, bustling with spring and filled with plans for the July Bathtub Race to Vancouver and the Highland Games that were part of the summer attractions. Still, as they explored the many antique shops, she was ever conscious of Paul's nearness, the slightest touch of his hand on her arm or shoulder sending wild shivers of promise through her veins.

It was nice to see that he had somehow managed to make peace with Barry by the time they left Nanaimo, for that eased the tension in the group. Joy treated Paul as she had before, being casually flirtatious and nothing more. Only Arianna was different, as much as she hated her reserve and the way it had replaced the moments of joyful ease they'd shared earlier.

Though Paul had mentioned the island where they were to have dinner, Arianna found herself full of questions once she and Joy left the boat rail to go down and change before they landed. "Where are we having dinner, Joy?" she asked as she poked through her small closet, wondering what she could wear that would appeal to Paul and also be casual, as he had suggested they dress simply and wear walking shoes.

Joy frowned. "I don't think he said. He mentioned an island and said that it would be different from the usual restaurants we visit on the tour, but I don't remember the name being mentioned."

"Do you think it's a surprise?" Arianna asked.

Her friend studied her with troubled eyes. "For whom?"

Arianna dropped her gaze to the tailored caramel linen slack suit that she'd taken from the closet. The dark brown knit top and the brown-caramel-and-orange scarf would make it feminine enough, she decided. She wondered even as she made her choice what exactly she was dressing for. Did she want to attract Paul, or was this the time to retreat from his forceful attention?

"What is going on, Arianna?" Joy asked, reminding her that she hadn't answered her friend's question.

She shrugged. "I don't know. He said he sent Tim away so that we'd have time to . . ." She couldn't go on. Her doubts clogged her throat.

"Does he really intend to marry you?" Joy asked.

"My father would never give his permission," Arianna answered, surprising herself. It was the first time she'd even thought about her father since she'd answered Paul's questions about him at the Morton Inn.

"You're eighteen."

Arianna swallowed hard. There didn't seem to be anything to say to that. "What are you going to wear?"

she inquired, changing the subject, refusing even to consider what Joy was suggesting.

"It's so romantic," Joy continued, undaunted. "Falling in love on this cruise. You could have your honeymoon on the *Star*, sailing from island to island, spending the moonlight nights on the most secluded beaches." She sighed with obvious envy.

Joy's words filled Arianna's mind with pictures that made her breath catch in her throat, and her hands shook a little as she pulled on the round-necked brown top and smoothed it into place over her slim hips. The things Joy was saying were what she'd been dreaming every night, she admitted to herself; the magic of love had dominated her thoughts since that first time on the beach.

A sharp knock on the door roused her from her reverie. "We're going to be landing in about twenty minutes," Barry called. "Are you two ready?"

"We'll be out in a few minutes," Joy answered. "Meet you on deck." She selected a navy suit with a ruffly blouse in three shades of pink.

They dressed without further conversation, but Arianna was conscious of Joy's questioning gaze from time to time, and she felt strangely guilty at being unable to share more of her feelings. They had been so close before, confiding everything in giggling conversations after the lights were out in the boarding-school dorm. But how could she confide what she didn't understand herself? How could she explain her longing and the fear that rose with it, the weakness that made her want to do anything Paul asked? Pehaps later, when she had made sense of her feelings.

"Ready?" Joy asked, breaking into her thoughts again.

Arianna smoothed her hair one last time. "As ready as I'll ever be, I guess," she answered, well aware that she was speaking of far more than the promised dinner.

"You'll draw all eyes," Joy told her. "Falling in love must agree with you. You seem to be blooming."

"In love?" Arianna looked at her friend for a moment, then left the cabin, hurrying ahead of Joy up the steps to the deck. It was a word she wasn't quite ready to confront.

"Ah, I'm glad you got here in time," Paul greeted her. His arm slid around her shoulders with such naturalness that she could only enjoy it. "I want you to see the island as we approach."

"What island is it?" Arianna asked, trying not to let her skipping heartbeat show in her voice.

"Pellington." His voice was soft and she could hear the love with which he spoke the word.

"The island the boat was named for?"

"The island where I was raised and where I still live when I'm not on the *Star*," Paul answered, turning her to face him instead of the rapidly approaching island. "I wanted you to see it, Arianna. I felt that it was important."

"I'm glad," Arianna murmured, her mouth dry again and her mind almost numbed by the implications of his words. "I'd like to see it all."

He caressed her cheek with his rough fingertips for just a moment; then they turned back toward the rail, his hands resting lightly on both her shoulders. "This is the village end of Pellington," he began, speaking louder now so that the Websters, Barry, and Joy could hear him too. "We'll tie up at the dock and explore the village for a little while; then we'll follow a path through the forest to a fishing camp at the other end of the island. Our dinner will be waiting for us there."

"A fishing camp?" Mrs. Webster asked, doubt plain in her tone.

"It's a very small place. A home converted to serving meals, several cabins for the fishermen who come to the island because of the abundance of fish in the waters around here. It's not as elegant as the last two resorts where we've eaten, but I can vouch for the talent of the cook."

There was a moment of silence; then Barry turned from the rail to look at Paul. "That wouldn't be the Roarke Camp, would it?" he asked.

"You must know a fisherman," Paul conceded with a grin.

"My uncle stayed there a couple of times. He was always promising to take me when I got older."

"You're taking us to your family's place?" Arianna was touched and intrigued by the idea.

"The cook is my mother," Paul admitted, "and she has promised a feast." His tone changed. "Now, ahead you can see an authentic fishing village, built up through the years. There are some small shops along the street, and a fisherman's tavern if shopping doesn't appeal. We'll meet in front of the tavern in about an hour for our walk to the fishing camp."

"Is it a long walk?" Mrs. Webster asked, her doubts still not allayed.

"Not very," Paul answered, "but if you don't wish to go, there's an excellent restaurant in the village. However, you'll have to be back on board before nine, as Mike will be bringing the *Star* to the other end of the island to pick us up and to anchor for the night."

"We'll let you know in an hour," Mr. Webster said.

"And I'll be with you in a few minutes, my love," Paul whispered to Arianna, his breath tickling in her ear as he bent to touch her neck with his lips for a moment before he went up to the bridge to bring the *Star* into the dock.

The moment Paul left, Joy was beside her. "So it is true," she gloated.

"What do you mean?" Arianna asked.

"Don't you know what this is all about?" Joy's tone was disbelieving. "He's brought you here to meet his parents. This trip wasn't on the tour itinerary. We were supposed to anchor all night at Nanaimo and have dinner there."

"Maybe he's just trying a new tour," Arianna murmured.

"For you." Joy's eyes were sparkling.

"Maybe we should do what the Websters are talking about and stay in town," Barry suggested, joining Joy. "Let our couple have a little privacy."

"Don't you dare!" Arianna gasped. "Joy, you wouldn't desert me now?"

Joy giggled. "If you could see your face," she teased.

Arianna took a deep breath and regained control of herself. "Please, Joy," she began, "it isn't funny. This is going too fast and I really need you to be with me tonight. I can't handle it alone."

Joy's expression softened and her hand was warm as she patted Arianna's arm. "Hey, we'll be with you, don't worry. I wouldn't miss it for the world. Barry was just teasing."

"I appreciate it."

"Don't let the pressure get to you," Joy advised. "There are only two more days on the tour, Arianna. After that, you can decide how far you want the relationship to go."

Arianna nodded, but without confidence. Her feelings for Paul went beyond logic or reason; she doubted that she would ever be able to deny her need for his touch, his kiss, the strange new magic that swept over her the moment they were together. Even more important, she wasn't sure that she wanted to deny it.

"Ready to go ashore, Arianna?" Paul asked, coming back to her now that the *Star* was secured to the dock.

"We're all ready," Joy answered with a smile.

The village was charming, with quaint old log buildings lining the single paved street. Most of the houses were two-story family dwellings with shops on the main floors and the curtained windows of apartments above. The restaurant and the local post office seemed to be the only two buildings devoted purely to business. There were approximately a dozen cabins and houses scattered on each end of the village. Beyond them, trees formed the edge of the wooded heart of the island.

"How could you ever leave this place?" Arianna asked as she stepped ashore. "It's beautiful and so peaceful."

"Unfortunately, that's the main drawback," Paul answered. "The peacefulness also means lack of opportunity. There just aren't any jobs on the island. Most of the kids go to the mainland or to Vancouver Island to school and just don't come back."

"Is that what you did?" Arianna asked.

"No, not really." Paul smiled down at her. "I was luckier. My father started the fish camp when I was just a kid, and I always had a job taking out the fishing parties. I still do when I don't have a charter for the *Star*."

"You take fishing parties on the *Star*?" Barry asked.

"Not since I've had it refitted," Paul replied. "It's too big for the kind of fishing most of the people at the camp want to do, so I just use one of my father's boats."

Barry looked as though he'd like to ask more questions, but before he could say anything, Paul began to talk about the shops and the restaurant, leading them along the narrow sidewalk to the center of town. "This is our local paper," he said, indicating a very untidy bulletin board that was carefully sheltered by plastic doors and an umbrella of bright rippled metal.

"Your what?" Arianna asked.

"This is where all notices are posted. The ferry schedules, lost and found, things for sale or rent, want ads, anything that anyone wants other people to know."

"You have a ferry that comes to this island?" Joy asked, surprised.

"Not a big one, like the ones that serve Seattle and Victoria and the other port cities, but a small one that hits all the little islands on a more or less regular basis," Paul explained, indicating a rather battered sheet of dates and times.

Arianna shook her head. "This all seems so strange," she admitted. "I mean, living on an island, having a ferryboat instead of a bus or train."

"It's a better way," Paul said, a special glint in his eyes as they met hers. His gaze was as intimate as a caress, almost a plea. "Things are slower here, but they give you a chance to enjoy life more. I come back as often as I can, when the cities get to me."

They wandered on, peering into the shops, sniffing appreciatively at the scents that wafted out the open door of the restaurant, then headed across the street to the tavern. It was not a large building, and the inside was dimly lit, the air filled with the smell of freshly popped corn and beer.

Mr. Webster stepped inside and looked at his wife. She nodded. "I think we'll leave you folks here," he said. "We'll make sure we're on the boat before nine."

"I've just walked too much today," Mrs. Webster said with a smile. "I shouldn't have tried to see all the antiques in Nanaimo."

"I'll tell Mike to expect you," Paul assured them, then added, "His family lives here in the village, so he'll be having dinner with them tonight."

Since there was no one to wait for, once they finished their tour of the village, Paul guided them past the bulletin board into the shadows of the trees beyond the cluster of houses. It was noticeably cooler once they stepped into the shady forest, and the path they followed was thick with wildflowers and tall grass.

"Don't you have any cars on the island?" Joy asked, looking around.

"Nowhere to drive them," Paul answered. "This is as close as we come to a road."

"But how do you move things?" Arianna asked.

"There are several motorcycles and a couple of snowmobiles for winter, plus two or three golf carts for hauling things from the village to the camp or vice versa."

Arianna looked around at the peaceful forest. The sun slanted through the thick pine boughs, highlighting tiny flowers and glinting off the dampness that still clung to the leaves of the wild roses. Her ears caught the whispered gurgle of a brook or stream, but she couldn't see it from the path.

Paul took her hand, holding it lightly but firmly. "I've always wanted to build my own cabin in the woods," he began, speaking softly. "There are some pretty meadows not too far from the camp that would be perfect—private, but not too lonely, especially later, when the camp becomes a real resort."

"Is that what you want, Paul?" Arianna asked, hearing something else in his voice, a kind of longing.

"That was always my dream," he replied. "A special retreat—good food, fishing, hiking, boating, a quiet place for people to find each other again."

Arianna looked up at him, sensing that there was something behind his words. She felt a pang, sure that he must, for the moment, be thinking of another love. She knew that a man his age must have had many loves.

"But enough of idle dreams," Paul said, his tone changing. "I'm a tour-boat captain and I'm not being a proper guide." He launched immediately into an easy recital of the history of Pellington Island, sprinkling the facts between amusing tales of the characters that had chosen this small, beautiful island to be their home. Arianna listened with rapt attention, wondering even as he spoke which of the people mentioned had been his ancestors.

Then, long before she was ready, the trees ended and a grassy verge stretched from them to a rustic old building. "And now, the moment you've all been waiting for," Paul concluded. "Dinner!"

"It's about time," Joy stated. "All this exercise is making me ravenous."

"Me too," Barry said. "And you look pretty tasty, lady."

Joy squealed as he pretended to be nibbling her neck, and Paul laughed at them, but Arianna was too uneasy to join in. There were a half-dozen chairs and benches on the wide porch of the main building, and several were occupied by casually dressed men of different ages.

One man got to his feet and called a greeting to Paul, but the others seemed uninterested as Paul led them up on the battered boards of the porch. "Just wait here," he said. "I'll go get my folks and introduce you before dinner."

Arianna winced as she felt Joy's elbow in her side. This couldn't be happening, she told herself. This was just another of her foolish dreams. In a minute she'd awaken and she'd be on the boat and Tim would be in the cabin across the passageway and they'd spend the day together and . . .

A soft, damp breeze caressed her hot cheeks and she licked her lips nervously. Her suit jacket, warm enough before, now seemed inadequate, and she was shivering even though her palms were damp.

"Arianna"—Paul's voice was warm—"come inside. Joy, Barry, you too."

Chapter Five

❧

The next few minutes were never clear in her mind. She had an impression of an older, dark-eyed version of Paul, who shook her hand so firmly her fingers ached, and a small, plump woman with laughing green eyes who hugged her as though welcoming her to far more than a dinner.

She tried to murmur the proper words, to pretend that it was just as it had been when her father took her places and introduced her to his important friends. However, she was terribly conscious of Paul's arm around her shoulders. Once again she felt smothered, cornered, rushed too fast.

"Now, how about a glass of white wine?" Paul suggested, breaking the spell.

"I'll have to leave you," Mrs. Roarke said. "But I am delighted that Paul has finally decided our camp is grand enough to be included in his tour."

"Mom, you know I just didn't want to spoil them for all the other places we go," Paul told her. "Nobody can compete with your cooking."

Her laughter filled the shabby but comfortable room. "With a compliment like that, I'd better get back to the kitchen," she told them. "We'll talk more later, Arianna. And welcome to Roarke Camp, all of you."

"Have you got a minute to look at something before dinner, son?" Mr. Roarke asked. "I've had a problem with the engine on the old *Pelican*."

"Will you excuse me, Arianna?" Paul asked, his eyes showing exasperation.

"Of course," Arianna assured him quickly, eager for a few minutes to gather her scattered wits. "May we look around a little?"

"Just don't get lost." His protective tone made her blush and she was sure that Mr. Roarke was staring at her, though she was too shy to meet his gaze.

"Let me get your wine," a slim woman in a waitress uniform offered as Paul and his father headed for the door. "Paul seems to be busy, as usual."

The cool, beaded wineglass felt good against her hot skin, and Arianna sipped it gratefully. The room was a treasure trove of photographs of fishermen and their catches, of boats in pictures and models done in loving detail. There were couches and chairs and love seats grouped in several friendly corners, and a small fire snapped and crackled appealingly in the large fireplace.

"Stop looking like you want to run away," Joy hissed in Arianna's ear.

"I can't."

Joy glared at her, then went over to where the waitress was fussing with things on what appeared to be a buffet table, though as yet very little food had been brought out. A half-dozen small tables were grouped near the big one, but none were occupied. Joy returned to Arianna's side and asked her to accompany her to the rest room.

"Look at yourself," Joy ordered, her tone furious.

Arianna turned to the mirror and gasped, understanding her friend's concern. Her eyes were huge and as frightened as a doe's and she looked about twelve in spite of the sophistication of her hairstyle and clothing.

"Is that what you want?" Joy continued. "Do you want him to see you as a little girl? I thought you were crazy about the guy, Arianna."

The shock and the sharp words were like a slap, and in the wake of it, life seemed to flood back into her. She took another sip of the wine that she'd carried with her, then began to repair her makeup with hands that were no longer shaking.

Joy watched her without a word, and finally nodded. "You look better," she told her at last. "What happened, anyway?"

"I guess I panicked," Arianna admitted. "Coming here, meeting his parents this way, it's all just too fast."

"If you were dating him in Denver, wouldn't you take him home to meet your father?" Joy asked.

"Well, of course, but . . ." Arianna let it trail off, then giggled. "I guess I am getting kind of wound up over nothing," she said after a moment. "I've just never felt this way about anyone before, and this place is so special, so beautiful."

"So let's go out and enjoy it. That is, of course, provided they feed us before I expire of starvation. If it tastes half as good as it smells, I may just stay."

With laughter, the spell was broken, and when they emerged, Arianna looked around with new eyes, enjoying the softly lit room with the snowy table linens. They studied the photographs hanging on the walls, adding their caustic comments to Barry's rather naughty observations about the fishermen pictured. By the time Paul returned, Arianna was even able to talk to his father without faltering.

The evening continued to glow like the candle lanterns that decorated the small tables. The buffet, a banquet from the sea and the gardens of vegetable growers, was finely cooked and a sheer pleasure to consume.

Food and wine loosened the tongues of the other guests, which included several women among the men anglers. Afterward there was music for dancing on the hastily cleared dining-room floor. Arianna was almost sorry when someone reported that the *Pellington Star* had just arrived and everyone went outside to watch as Mike secured it to the dock.

Since the fishermen had left early, pleading dawn dates with fish, Arianna suggested to Paul that they return to the *Star* even though she felt a great reluctance to end the evening. Joy and Barry were already strolling along the dock, their arms around each other, when she paused in the path to look back at the building.

"So that's where you grew up," she murmured, trying to picture him as a little boy here.

"Would you like to see my home now?" Paul asked, his fingers moving tenderly on the back of her neck beneath the heavy fall of her hair.

"Your home?"

"Come on, it's not too late. Just because everyone else turns in with the chickens doesn't mean we have to. I don't want this evening to end." He drew her into his arms, his lips finding hers before she could say anything.

Excitement shivered through her, rousing feelings that had grown more intense now that she knew Paul better. She clung to him eagerly, wanting the moment to last forever, hating the thought of her narrow, empty bunk.

"I don't live in the camp itself," Paul continued when their lips parted. "Once I got out of college, I wanted a place of my own, so I built it. Come on, I'll show you."

Intrigued with this picture of the man she now felt she loved, Arianna snuggled close to his side and quickened her steps to keep pace with his long-legged stride. He led her into the shadows of the forest that grew on three sides of the cleared area.

"It's so dark," Arianna gasped as the trees swallowed them, shutting out the moon and the stars that had made the lapping water polished silver and the grass a velvet carpet.

"Your eyes will adjust," Paul told her, his embrace tightening. "Not that I need to see to find my way. I've walked this path since I was a little boy."

Her feet found the smoother ground, and the darkness resolved itself into shadowy outlines of trees and bushes. Arianna rested her cheek against the rough fabric of his jacket, loving the privacy of this place, the magic of sharing it with Paul.

"There's a meadow over that way," he said, pointing to where she could see a silvery lighted area between the dark bulk of the trees, "and the cabin is this way."

The cabin was merely a darker shadow than the trees, but when she stumbled up the steps and followed Paul inside, she could feel the warmth of the air, smell the musty scent of neglect and dust that rose around them. She hesitated then, suddenly a little frightened to be here alone with Paul.

"Shall I light a candle?" he asked, his voice as soft and hushed as the light breeze had been.

"I can't see it if you don't," she teased, trying to lift the tension that she could feel building between them.

"There's not much to see," he whispered, his lips moving along her neck, his warm breath causing sensations that brought gooseflesh to her arms. "But there will be, I promise, Arianna. This was just a haven for me, but it could be a real home."

The implications of the statement really shocked her, but his lips were already on hers. His tongue tickled the corner of her mouth; then his lips claimed hers in a kiss that absorbed her whole being in the wild delight that radiated from her mouth to her quivering body.

His embrace was crushing; then it loosened and his hand slipped inside her jacket to caress her, sliding beneath the soft knit top to find her breast. A shiver traveled through her at the touch. As she felt the nipple harden beneath his fingers, a new sensation traveled through her entire body in some mysterious way.

"I love you, Arianna," he whispered, his hands moving to slip her jacket off, then easing her knit top up so that his lips could move down toward her breast.

"Paul," she gasped, her whole body suddenly weak with the new emotions that he was unleashing.

He guided her through the darkness and eased her down tenderly onto a bed. For a moment she was too shocked to protest; then she felt her top being removed, her lacy bra stripped away.

"Paul, no, I . . ."

"I won't hurt you, my love," he said, moving away for a moment. She felt the bed shift as his weight settled beside her.

His hands found her freed breasts and began their magic again. She tried to push him away and felt only his skin, soft with the dark hair that grew on his chest. His arms slid around her again and his mouth sought hers as he pulled her body to his, her sensitively roused nipples slowly flattening against the hardness of his chest.

It couldn't be happening. It was wrong! She had to stop. The thoughts roared through her mind, but her body was oblivious as she moved even closer, feeling his hand on her hips as he brought her hard against him, letting her feel the swelling heat of his desire. It frightened and excited her even more as his kisses subdued her will to resist.

The crash was like a thunderbolt following the lightning that was crackling between them. Paul rolled away from her with a curse, stumbled to his feet, and moved in the direction of the door he'd left open. Chilled by the rush of cold air that flowed over her naked breasts, Arianna struggled to sit up. Her body felt as though it were made of honey, too fluid and warm to do more than absorb the wild joy that had been flaming between them.

Arianna shivered, filled with embarrassment and shame as she realized what was happening. She sought through the darkness for her clothing, finding her top and jacket, but not her bra. She donned them quickly, her hands shaking.

Suddenly hands touched her shoulders. "What are you doing?" Paul demanded, his voice rough with his feelings. "It was just the wind banging a branch against the cabin. There's a squall blowing up. It's going to be raining soon."

"We have to get back to the boat," Arianna answered, embarrassed at the way her voice quivered.

"We'll be safe enough here." Paul pulled her to him, and she felt the languid honey returning to make her knees as weak as her resolve to stop what was happening.

"No," she repeated, pulling away from his questing fingers. "I can't stay here with you, Paul."

His embrace became gentle. "Don't be afraid of me, little Arianna," he whispered, his lips against her neck. "You want me as much as I want you, and I promise to be gentle. I'd never hurt you, you must know that."

"Please, no, Paul." Her protests sounded feeble even to her ears, and she felt his hand fumbling once again beneath her knit top, seeking her unprotected breast. One more moment and she'd be beyond refusal, beyond anything but the maddening excitement of the unknown delights his touch promised and her traitorous body seemed to yearn for.

"No!" Her slap sounded louder than the crash of the wind-driven branch had, and even before she felt the stinging of her palm, another pain stabbed through her.

Paul's hands and arms dropped from her, leaving her free, but taking her heart with him. For a minute she tried to find words to explain, to tell him that it wasn't his advances, but her own responses, that frightened her. But no words came, and in the end, panic drove her toward the dim world outside and she fled into the wind-swirling night. It was a nightmare. The wind buffeted her and the pines seemed to be reaching

out their sticky-needled boughs to grab her wildly flowing hair or to snag in her jacket. She stumbled over the
rough ground, terrified of pursuit, of being lost, of
having to face Paul and explain her weakness.

By the time she broke free of the woods and staggered
past the cabins, her heart was pounding like thunder in
her ears and each breath brought a fresh stab of pain
from her side. Sobbing, she forced her shaking legs to
carry her toward the boat, praying that all aboard would
be in bed or seeking shelter from the rapidly approaching storm.

Raindrops chased her the last few steps along the
dock, and she ran across the deck to dive into the
darkness of the passageway without even looking back.
She didn't stop till she reached her cabin door. To her
surprise, Joy pulled it open even before she touched
the knob.

"Arianna, what in the world?" Joy's eyes went over
her, widening as they cataloged the disheveled hair,
twisted clothing, the obvious lack of a bra under the
knit top. "What happened?" she asked, much more
quietly.

A thousand answers filled her mind, but when her
mouth opened, she could only sob. Joy's arms slipped
around her shoulders, comforting her. "Did he hurt
you, Arianna? What happened? Where is Paul?"

Arianna closed her eyes. "He took me to his cabin in
the woods and he . . . he tried to make love to me, Joy."

The brunette lifted an eyebrow. "You shouldn't be
that surprised, Arianna," she reminded her. "He hasn't
exactly made a secret of the way he feels, and he's not a
kid." She frowned. "Did he force you or . . . or anything?"

Arianna shook her head, remembering Paul's tenderness, his promise never to hurt her. She was suddenly embarrassed by her own actions. She'd come so close to yielding, a man of his experience must have known how she felt, and then to strike out at him like a hysterical child . . .

"What did happen?" Joy asked.

"I can't stay here, Joy," Arianna said instead of answering. "I can't face him again, not after tonight."

"But if he loves you—"

"He doesn't, not now. He'll hate me." The panic was rising again, but not for the reasons she was stating. A deeper instinct told her that Paul wouldn't give up so easily, and she knew beyond a doubt that she'd never be able to stop herself again.

"You can't run away," Joy told her. "You have to face this."

"No, you have to help me. I can't stay here tonight. I have to get off the boat now and run away before he . . ." She stopped, hearing the sound of footsteps outside her door.

The tap was light but firm. "Arianna, are you all right?" Paul's voice held only concern.

Joy looked at Arianna, waiting for her reply, but she couldn't speak. His very nearness froze her with the wild emotions it sent flooding through her. He knocked again, louder.

"She's here, Paul," Joy called out, "but she doesn't want to talk to you now."

There was a silence from the other side of the door, and Arianna held her breath, half-expecting Paul simply to open the door and come in to claim her. That thought filled her with something much closer to excitement than fear.

"I'll be here tomorrow, Arianna," he said at last. "We'll talk when you're feeling better."

Arianna let her breath out slowly as she heard his feet retreating along the passageway to his quarters. She lifted a shaking hand to smooth back the tangled fall of her hair.

"He's not kidding, Arianna," Joy whispered. "There's no way he's going to let you off this boat without a confrontation."

Arianna nodded, taking several deep breaths and beginning to think instead of react. "That's why I have to leave now," she explained. "I really can't face him, Joy. It would be a disaster. I have to have time to think, to sort out what happened."

Her friend didn't look convinced. "Where will you go?" she asked. "This is his island, you know."

"The interisland ferry," Arianna answered, her plan forming even as she spoke. "I can walk to the village later, after everyone is asleep. I can hide in that empty barn we passed, and catch the morning ferry. You can just pretend I'm sleeping till after you sail. He won't have to know till noon, and by then I'll be somewhere he can't find me."

"But where?" Joy shook her head. "There's only two days left on the tour, Arianna. I can't go home without you. My father would kill me, and so would your father."

"Isn't there somewhere else you could stay for a couple of days?" Arianna asked. "I don't want to go to your house till I'm sure Paul won't go there."

Joy sighed. "I suppose I could visit my Aunt Meg in Vancouver for a couple of days. Daddy would probably believe that. I guess I could say that I wanted to show you that part of the country too. But, Arianna, what will you do?"

"I'll stay on some other island for a day or so, then meet you in Vancouver," Arianna answered. "I just need a little time alone, to think." She hoped fervently that it was true, that a couple of days away from Paul would somehow end the violent feelings that still surged through her the moment she even heard his name.

Joy looked as though she'd like to argue further, but Arianna forestalled it by taking out her little overnight case. She packed only the necessities, then changed her clothes, dressing as warmly as she could and taking out the bright raincoat that she'd brought along but had had no use for until now. Her hair she simply brushed back, making a single heavy braid that she tied with a scarf.

The girl that looked back at her from the mirror was somewhat of a stranger with her pale, bruised mouth and red-rimmed brown eyes reflecting her pain. A few short wisps of golden hair had escaped her braid and curled about her face, but they couldn't soften the impression that the girl had aged suddenly and painfully.

"Where can I reach you?" Joy asked.

"You can't. I don't even know where the ferry goes, I just remember seeing on the schedule that it comes by about six-thirty in the morning. I thought it was early." Her smile was wry. "Give me your aunt's name and phone number and I'll call you as soon as I get to Vancouver."

"Call me from wherever you are," Joy told her. "I'll be worried, Arianna. I really don't think this is a good idea. If you want to stay away from Paul, just tell him so. I'm sure he isn't the type to force himself on a girl."

Arianna picked up her case and coat, then looked around the cabin, wondering if she was forgetting something important. "Just pack up what's left," she told Joy. "I'm sorry to be such a coward, but I can't face him—not now."

"Well, I could tell him that ..." Joy stopped, then asked, "Why do you hate him so much?"

Arianna's smile was tinged with bitterness. "I don't hate him. I have to leave because I'm crazy in love with him and I can't bear to be on the same boat and not ..." She couldn't finish, for her throat closed as memories of his touch washed over her. She gave a feeble flutter of her fingers, then eased the cabin door open and peered out into the passageway.

The boat was quiet and appeared empty. It rocked more than usual as the wind buffeted it and stirred the waves. Arianna climbed the steps to the deck, then stayed undercover surveying the scene while she pulled on her raincoat and secured the hood tightly against the wind. The falling rain mingled with her tears as she ran away.

Chapter Six

The rain continued to plague her all the way to the abandoned barn. Once inside, when she decided to lie down, she had to be careful to choose a pile of straw away from the many leaks that dripped from the roof. It was cold and miserable, yet she almost welcomed the discomfort. When she thought of the cold and damp and the hardness of the ground beneath the prickly straw, she could almost forget those moments in Paul's arms, in his bed.

What would he think when he discovered that she was gone? she wondered, then hated herself for the weakness that such thoughts betrayed. She was going to forget him, so what did it matter what he thought? A burst of hysterical laughter filled her throat, but changed to sobs as it came out. How could she ever forget him when he filled her senses so completely that she could think of nothing else?

It was a brief and miserable night and she knew that she looked almost as awful as she felt when she made her way to the town dock to buy a ticket on the ferry. "Where to?" the sleepy-eyed attendant asked.

Arianna eyed the list despairingly, not knowing what to answer. The last name caught her eye and she said it quickly, hoping he wouldn't notice her confusion.

"End of the line, huh," the attendant observed. "It's a pretty place. Got a small hotel and some nice shops. You'll enjoy it."

Arianna nodded and forced a smile. "All the islands are beautiful," she began, then had to stop as she thought that this island was the loveliest of all because it was Paul's island. She took her ticket and left, wishing now that she'd chosen a closer destination, for she'd forgotten how limited her funds were. She had credit cards, of course, but some places might not take them.

Though she tried to concentrate on such mundane thoughts for the next half-hour, she had trouble keeping her eyes away from the path that led to the fishing camp. Somehow she kept expecting to see Paul striding out of the trees, seeking her. She was almost disappointed when the ferry arrived to unload its daily cargo and take on the goods and passengers that were traveling to other islands.

The trip was endless. People came and went, many friendly or curious, but she was unable to respond to any of them beyond mere politeness. Exhaustion dragged at her, and it wasn't until late afternoon that she realized that she'd had nothing to eat since the sumptuous feast at the fish camp. She was glad to go ashore at the last stop.

The small hotel was nicer than she'd expected. Like others she'd seen on the tour, it was an old house converted to accommodate guests, but this one was especially homey and comfortable. The woman who stepped out from behind the ornate desk was motherly and Arianna had no trouble allowing herself to be shown to a room so she could clean up, with the promise of dinner being served as soon as she came back down to the dining room.

Food revived her, ending the dizzy vagueness that had haunted her since morning, but with clarity of thought came more painful memories. Every moment of last night played through her mind like a movie, only her body still felt his touch, his heat, his matching desire. Had there been an easy way to reach the *Pellington Star*, she knew she would have surrendered to her love and gone to him, beyond denying her passionate need.

After her early dinner, she wandered aimlessly about the beautiful town, too restless to return to her room, though she was exhausted. She tried to think logically about Paul, about what had happened, but she felt only the agony of his absence. For the first time in weeks she longed for her home, for the safety of Denver and all that she'd known there. Yet a part of her mind told her that it would never be the same, for now she was not the same.

Depressed and weary, she found her way back to the hotel and retreated to her small room. A long hot bath eased some of the ache from her bones, and she washed and dried her hair before she finally surrendered to her exhaustion and collapsed into what felt suspiciously like a feather bed.

After going to bed early, Arianna found herself wide-awake at dawn. Knowing from the notice on the battered antique dresser in her room that breakfast would not be served for several hours, she tried to go back to sleep, but without success. Haunted by her memories and unable to bear the emptiness of the world without Paul, she got up and pulled on the jeans and T-shirt that she'd packed that confusing night.

She was busily brushing her hair, trying to decide whether to braid it again or to tie it back with the scarf, when she heard a knock on her door. Frowning, she hesitated for a moment, not sure who could be outside so early. The knock came again, harder this time. Sighing, she went over and opened the door.

Paul stood in the hall, looking larger than she remembered. His dark hair was tousled by the wind and his face had the stern angry look of a man on a quest. Arianna gasped and tried to slam the door, but he seemed to sense her purpose, for he was inside before she could shut the door.

"Not this time, Arianna," he said softly, closing the door behind him. He moved a chair over so that he could sit in front of the door, effectively making her his prisoner.

"You can't keep me here," Arianna protested.

"And you can't leave before we talk," Paul answered calmly.

"How did you find me?" Arianna started to sit on the bed, then trembled at the memory of another bed and all that had happened there. She retreated farther to the padded window seat, ignoring the cold air that swirled in from outside.

"It wasn't difficult once I found out that you'd left the boat." His stern expression softened, letting her see the vulnerable, hurt man behind it. "Why, Arianna? What did you think I'd do to you? You didn't have to fight me off. I told you that I'd never hurt you, and I meant that. I love you and I think that you love me. Can you deny that?"

She tried to, but under the pressure of his stern green-eyed stare, she couldn't lie. "It's too soon, Paul, too fast. What happened in the cabin . . . I couldn't face you. I needed time to think. My life has been planned for years, and now I'm not sure of anything. Please don't hate me." Words were inadequate. She couldn't explain that she loved him, yet feared the very strength of her desire for him.

"I could never hate you, Arianna. I just didn't understand how innocent you are. That's why I wanted to talk to you, to explain what happened."

"There's nothing to say." Arianna turned away, her eyes unfocused as she faced the scene beyond the window. Suddenly she thought of Joy and the *Star*. "How did you get here?" she asked. "Where are Joy and the others?"

"They're enjoying their cruise on the *Star*," Paul answered. "Luckily, I insisted on seeing you as soon as Joy came out of the cabin. When I saw that your bunk hadn't been slept in, I had Mike put me ashore on Pellington. It didn't take long to find out what you'd done. Bob, the ticket salesman on the dock, remembered you perfectly. I just followed in the *Pelican*."

"You should have let me go," she told him, aware that she could never bear it if he did.

"How could I?" he asked, his tone so filled with emotion that she had to look at him. "We belong together, Arianna. You felt it last night just as I did. It frightened you, but you'll learn to trust your own feelings in time. I'll help you to learn. But I won't let you go, not ever. I've searched all my life for you, no* knowing who you were or what you'd be like. I'm just glad that I've found you at last."

The words sang through her, easing the doubts, thrilling her with the promise they whispered to her. He was on his feet now, moving closer, so near that she could feel the heat of his body and smell the spiciness of his after-shave.

"We'll be married in two hours," he continued, his lips moving over her eyes, her cheeks, touching her nose, then finding her mouth as the shock of his words swept over her. When his lips released hers, she could only look up at him, too happy to speak.

"It's a special license and it took a couple of friends to get it, but I wanted to have it to offer when I found you. I wanted you to know that what I feel for you is forever, Arianna, and to ask you if you can make the same commitment."

Her doubts were gone as their eyes met. She remembered the agony of last night's flight and knew that it had been wrong. Her heart was Paul's already; there could be no question about following it. "I love you," she whispered before she lifted her lips to meet his.

"I've made all the arrangements," Paul continued when they paused to catch their breath, "even for our wedding breakfast, which is probably on the table downstairs by now."

"I should wait for my father . . ." she began half-heartedly.

"If you want a big ceremony for your father and your friends, we can have it later," Paul told her, his arms tightening possessively. "I don't mind marrying you as many times as you want, but the first time is going to be today, and we are going to spend our honeymoon on the *Pelican*. I'll teach you about love, my darling little Arianna, and I promise you'll never be tempted to run away from me again."

Joy bubbled up in her throat and she found herself laughing and crying as she answered his kiss. "I know that," she whispered against his lips. "Never again."

The next two hours passed in a blur as Mrs. Kootz, the owner of the hotel and an old friend of Paul's family, took over management of the wedding. While they ate the huge breakfast she'd prepared, she made plans to hold the wedding in the ornate parlor of the hotel, bringing in her own spring flowers to brighten the room.

"Now, you come with me, Arianna," she ordered as soon as they finished eating. "You can't wear jeans for your wedding."

Arianna followed Mrs. Kootz for a fast trip up three flights of stairs to the dim and dusty attic. Her hostess began rooting through the trunks and after several frantic minutes produced a faded blue box. "Come along," she ordered, dragging Arianna back down to what was apparently her room. "Try this on."

The dress was old, its once-white folds golden with time. But it was still beautiful with its tiny embroidered roses and bows, seed pearls, and satin touches. Exquisitely styled with a sweetheart neck edged with lace and pearls, it fit snugly about her tiny waist, then fell in formal folds to the floor.

"Was this yours?" Arianna gasped, touching the material reverently.

"And my mother's before me," Mrs. Kootz answered, then sighed. "I'd hoped to have a daughter to wear it, but I was given only four great hulking boys, and their brides were all too plump or too short or too tall. And mostly far too modern to want to wear such an old-fashioned gown."

"How could anyone resist something so lovely?" Arianna breathed, daring to look at her reflection in the mirror and gasping to see how it transformed her. "But I couldn't ask to borrow this."

"You didn't," Mrs. Kootz reminded her. "I offered, and I'm delighted to see it worn once again, and by someone who looks as lovely as you do."

"I'll never be able to thank you enough."

"Make Paul happy," Mrs. Kootz answered. "He's been a good boy, but he needs someone to settle him down. His poor mother was beginning to be afraid he'd never find the right girl."

Arianna managed to continue to smile, though she couldn't help wondering how Mrs. Roarke would feel once she learned of the wedding. And her own father? She swallowed hard, aware that Paul was even now sending the telegram she'd composed to her father.

Her father would be furious, she was sure, and hurt. But once she'd explained and he'd met Paul, surely he'd see that they were perfect for each other. Then he'd understand.

"What do you think of this for your veil?" Mrs. Kootz asked, reclaiming her attention as she lifted a drift of old lace from the box. "The crown I wore with it is long gone, but perhaps with a wreath of fresh flowers? Your hair is crown enough."

It was more than a little bit like a dream as she was dressed and fussed over. With her hair expertly smoothed to frame her suddenly glowing face, the wreath of flowers, all pink and white rosebuds, was perfect to secure the veil. When she had a moment to touch her makeup and get a final glimpse of herself in the old mirror, she knew that for once she was truly beautiful.

The ceremony was simple but full of tender promises that she made in a voice that shook only a little. Then suddenly Paul was slipping a wide gold band on her finger and bending to kiss her with gentle passion.

Champagne corks popped and the half-dozen people from the hotel joined them in drinking toasts to the future and the wonder of love. Then it was time for her to change out of the glorious gown and return to reality. Feeling a bit like Cinderella after midnight, Arianna kept her wreath in her hair as she donned her jeans and T-shirt. She felt a pang of regret that she should be going on her honeymoon with so little that would please this exciting stranger who was now her husband.

Calling profuse thanks to Mrs. Kootz, they fled from the hotel in a blizzard of rice. It was half a block before Paul slowed and she could ask, "Where do we go now?"

His smile was a caress. "Unromantic as it may sound, I think we'd better make a stop at the grocery store. I didn't have time to get provisions for the *Pelican* before I came after you, and the places we're going don't exactly have a store on every corner."

"Where are we going?" Arianna asked.

"My little corner of paradise."

And so it proved to be.

The *Pelican* was a much smaller version of the *Star*. An older boat, dating from a day when time was taken to produce fine wood and handsome brass, the craft had a feeling of opulence. Though outfitted for fishing, the owner's cabin was well-cared-for and boasted a double bunk instead of the customary twin bunks that were in the other cabin. Arianna blushed when she saw it, yet she felt no urge to run away.

They sailed from the island as soon as things were stowed aboard. Smiling, Arianna hid the box containing the nightgown that she'd slipped away to purchase, pleased that she'd taken the time while Paul was in the grocery store. It wasn't the concoction of French silk and lace that she would have chosen had she been at home, but she had a feeling that Paul wouldn't mind a bit. It was, at least, more romantic than the flannel nightshirt that she'd brought with her from the *Star*.

Once they were out of the harbor, Paul called her to the bridge and began to show her the art of guiding the boat as it rode lightly over the waves. It seemed surprisingly casual and natural, not at all the way she had expected her honeymoon to be. He held her lightly, kissing her occasionally and nuzzling her free-blowing hair, but there was none of the urgency she'd sensed in the forest cabin.

"What happens next?" she asked after they left the land far behind. "Are you going to teach me to fish?"

He released her, stepping back so that he could look into her eyes. "Is that what you really want to do?" he asked solemnly.

"I thought maybe it was what you wanted to do," she teased.

"Actually, I thought we might have a picnic on a certain beach," he told her. "It's a small island, just a speck that really doesn't belong to anyone that I know of. It's uninhabited and not close enough to any other islands to be visited often, but it's very lovely and private and the cove is just big enough for us to anchor the *Pelican* and spend the night."

"Our own little island," Arianna breathed, entranced with the idea.

"Our own private world," Paul corrected, pulling her close so that he could kiss her slowly and deeply, as though he wanted to make every corner and curve of her mouth his own.

When he let her go, she had to lean against the side of the boat, her knees weak with desire, her heart pounding with the passion and love he'd taught her. It was several minutes before she caught her breath enough to ask, "Should I go down and fix something for our picnic?"

"It's all packed and waiting," he informed her with a grin. "A wedding gift from Mrs. Kootz."

"I already owe her so much for our wedding," Arianna murmured. "Letting me wear that gorgeous gown and everything she did. If it hadn't been for her, I'd have had to marry you in these." She waved a hand at her faded but perfectly fitted designer jeans.

"Do you really think it mattered to me?" he asked, his green eyes glinting. "I would have married you even without your jeans."

She giggled, not minding her blush as his arms tightened around her again. "In fact," he continued, "I might have preferred you that way."

They continued to chat easily as another hour sped by. Then one of the silences that rested so contentedly between them was interrupted by the low rumble of her stomach. Arianna giggled nervously. "I guess I should have eaten more breakfast," she murmured.

"We'll be there in about fifteen or twenty minutes,"

Paul assured her. "See that little island just off to the left?" He pointed. "That's Roaring Rock Island."

"What?" Arianna was intrigued by the name.

"Roaring Rock. I've always said the name was bigger than the island, but it comes from the fact that the cliffs on the far side have been cut away by the wind so that when there's a gale, they sound like a cage full of lions at feeding time. Of course, not too many people have anchored there in a storm, so most maps don't even show a name for it."

They circled the island and Arianna searched the rocky cliffs and thickly forested shore for signs of life, but there were none. The inlet to the tiny cove was so narrow the larger *Pellington Star* clearly wouldn't have been able to enter.

The cove itself was larger than she'd expected, and screened from the wind by the tall evergreens that grew nearly to the edge of the land surrounding the placid blue water. Paul cut the motor, and the sudden silence was a shock to ears conditioned to the throb of an engine.

"What do you think of our private paradise, Arianna?" Paul asked, his eyes searching her face as though he was truly unsure of her response.

"It's almost as beautiful as your island," she told him. She turned away to survey the shore, which was sandy between the outcroppings of rock. "And wonderfully private."

"Let me drop the anchor; then we'll swim ashore."

"Swim?"

"Don't you know how to swim?" Paul asked, shock plain on his suntanned features.

"I don't have my swimming suit," Arianna admitted. "I left it on the *Star* with all my other clothes."

A slow smile spread over Paul's face and his eyes caressed her. "Well, now, as it happens, I didn't bother to bring one either," he said. "What do you say we just put our clothes in the little raft and swim across without them?"

For a moment she hesitated, feeling frightened and shy, but then she saw the challenge in his eyes. "If we have a raft, why do we have to swim?" she asked.

Paul grinned. "Because some idiot forgot the oars in his rush, and we'd starve to death before we could paddle the thing to shore with our hands."

She giggled. "And I thought you were always prepared," she teased. "A captain who forgets his oars . . ." She shook her head in mock despair.

Suddenly she was lifted in his arms and he was striding purposefully toward the rail of the boat. "As you were saying . . ." he began, holding her out over the dancing water.

Arianna looked down, then wrapped her arms around his neck. "Wouldn't you rather keep me here?" she asked as she pressed her lips to his.

She was barely conscious of being moved back, of the ease with which he allowed her body to slide down to melt against his. They were both breathing hard when his embrace finally loosened and he stepped away, shaking his head. "Keep that up and we won't make it to shore," he warned hoarsely.

For a moment she thought of the wide bunk; then her stomach rumbled again. "And miss my wedding picnic? Never. Where is it? I'll bring it up while you get the raft and drop anchor or whatever you have to do."

He chuckled. "The basket is in the galley. And bring the champagne that's in the refrigerator. We'll have a picnic to end all picnics. And a blanket from the spare cabin."

Arianna hurried to obey, grunting a little in shock at the weight of the basket. She could hardly carry it, the bottles, and the blanket at the same time and was glad when Paul came to help. He took the basket and one bottle of champagne, leading the way to the stern of the boat, where a small rubber raft was tethered.

Once things were lowered to the bouncing raft, he turned to Arianna, his eyes once again blazing a challenge as he unbuttoned his shirt and spread it on the deck, using it to hold his shoes and the soft caramel slacks he'd been wearing. He paused then, clad only in brief shorts that fit superbly. She felt her breath quicken at the hard-lined beauty of his sculptured form. The muscles rippled smoothly beneath his tanned skin and she could see the dark furry line that moved from the thick mat of hair on his chest to disappear beneath the waistband of his shorts.

"Will you come with me, Arianna?" he asked, not moving toward her, though his eyes caressed her.

For a moment she was afraid; then slowly she pulled off her T-shirt and slipped off her jeans, removing her canvas deck shoes at the same time. She felt almost naked in the wispy lace bra that confined but didn't truly cover her swelling breasts, and the dainty lace-trimmed pink panties that were only a shade deeper than her pale skin.

His eyes touched her body again, then lifted to meet her eyes, holding her gaze as he stripped off his shorts, dropped them on the shirt, then turned and jumped lightly into the water beside the raft. "Just put your things in the shirt, tie the whole thing together with the sleeves, and hand it down to the raft," he ordered. "Then untie the rope and come on, if you want anything to eat."

Her hands were shaking as she unhooked her bra, and they were icy against her skin as she shed her panties, but she forced herself to stand straight and proud as she carried the clothes to the open section of rail and lowered them to the raft. She didn't look his way as she untied the rope, but when she tossed it to him, she could see the pleasure in his face and she felt no shyness as she dived in beside him.

The icy touch of the water nearly sent her back up to the boat deck, but once she started to swim, the blood returned to her skin. As she drew alongside Paul, the heat of her love for him warmed her even more. He guided her to the shore, pushed the raft up on a ledge of rock and then put the champagne back into the water.

Arianna started to wade ashore, but his hands caught her around the waist and he pulled her back into the gently lapping water, holding her close against his body. When the water was to her shoulders, he began to swim slowly around her, his body a sleek caress as it touched hers.

It was several minutes before he allowed his feet to settle to the bottom again and drew her into an embrace that encompassed her entire body. His hands moved over her back and hips in long, sensuous strokes as his kiss banished the cold water in a burning rush of passionate need. After what seemed a lifetime, he picked her up, and without releasing her lips, carried her out of the water, across the tiny scrap of shore, and into a tree-shadowed bower.

"My love," he whispered, laying her gently on the long, sweet-scented grass. "My beautiful, beautiful love."

His hands moved over her, his lips trailing them as though to kiss and taste every inch of her quivering skin. Never had she felt such excitement. Her own hands explored timidly, seeking to know his body as he seemed to know hers. Then came the moment when the wild delight was almost beyond bearing, and she could move no closer to him.

"Love me, Paul," she sobbed. "Oh, love me, please."

The trees and the grass vanished as she became a part of him—their labored breathing, pounding hearts, and straining eager bodies one. It lasted forever and yet could never be long enough, and when it was over, she could only lie still and wonder if she'd ever know such happiness again.

Paul said nothing, but she felt his hands gently stroking her, a tender easing back from the drowning wonder of what they'd shared. He waited till her eyes opened and she looked at him; then he grinned, his eyes gleaming wickedly. "And I thought you said you were hungry," he teased.

The rush of shared laughter banished the momentary awkwardness, and Arianna followed him to the sea to wash off the grass and the marks of their passion without shame. She was a woman who knew the bounds of a woman's joy; it was a magic moment and the beginning of the happiest time of her life.

Chapter Seven

Arianna sat up, forcing the memories away even as she became aware that her breath was coming fast and her hands were cold and damp. Five years, and she still felt the same throbbing love and desire just thinking about him. It was madness, just as her father had said when he'd come after her.

"Temporary insanity," he'd called it, blaming her youth and innocence and calling Paul terrible things.

They'd had less than two weeks together after that first wonderful afternoon, but what a golden time it had been. Twelve magical days of sailing between the beautiful green islands, anchoring in jewel-like inlets, swimming in the secret coves that Paul always managed to find, picnicking on the deserted beaches, kissing, touching, making love.

In that time Paul had taken her from the breathless innocence of that first time to the magnificent tempest of true loving passion. He'd taught her the strength of her own beauty and given her an understanding of the power of vulnerability. He'd made her a woman and then . . .

She shivered, not because she was cold, but because she was lost, because she had been lost to herself ever since her father had found her and ended her marriage. The fact that he'd proved that Paul Roarke was nothing more than a fortune hunter had negated all the magic and made her doubt herself once again.

But now she knew that the marriage hadn't actually ended. In spite of all the terrible things her father had said about Paul, he hadn't gone through with securing the annulment. Had Paul stopped him? Why? And why hadn't her father told her that the marriage was still a fact?

Arianna looked out at the green grandeur of the Colorado Rockies and sighed. Could her father have been wrong about Paul five years ago? It was a question she'd asked herself a thousand times as she toured Europe with her father. But her father had had all the answers then—Paul's failure to try to reach her, the separation agreement that had arrived so promptly.

Her eyes left the scenery and moved back to the picture that smiled at her from her dressing table. Her father, handsome, dynamic, more exciting than any man she'd dated before or after Paul came into her life. She felt a familiar surge of love, but this time it was well washed with pain. How could the man she'd loved and trusted all her life be the man who'd betrayed her and all his friends and business associates?

Had she ever known him at all? Had she ever known any man at all? Paul a fortune hunter bought off so easily; the other men she had seen slipping out of her life almost unnoticed; her father creating a financial scandal that would only grow worse according to Mr. Potter. Was the fault theirs ... or hers? It was a question she couldn't answer, but the immensity of her pain told Arianna that she must find the answer if she was ever to have a chance to love again.

"Miss Arianna, are you going to want dinner soon?" The housekeeper's voice forced her to return to the present, to banish the past joys and sorrows so that she could face the ones that loomed even closer.

Two horrible days inched by. After the official announcement of the collapse of Kane Investments, the phone rang constantly and the doorbell frequently. Arianna soon learned not to answer either one, for the callers were mostly reporters, and she had no explanations for them. She had no explanations for herself.

Mrs. Cranston, the housekeeper who had cared for her since her mother's death twenty years earlier, dealt with all the callers, her face stern and hard. She and Arianna had never been close, but now that their safe world was ending, she was surprisingly protective and concerned.

"Mr. Kane should have made better provisions for you," she said with amazing frequency. "All those years he took such good care of you, I just don't understand it."

Arianna could only shake her head, wishing, too, that her father had shown more care in both his business and personal life. Yet in the very depths of this isolation, she began to find her strength. She disposed of the problems left by her father: cataloging, locating papers and facts. She handled everything that came up as unemotionally as if it were happening to someone else.

Mr. Potter called her the third morning. "Do you

have some news about Paul?" she asked after they'd exchanged greetings.

"I've located Mr. Roarke," he replied. "He's living on Pellington Island. That's off the coast of—"

"I know where it is," Arianna interrupted, remembering it all too clearly. "Do you have any information about my legal status?" That was the hard question to ask.

"I've found no record of a divorce or of any new marriage licenses being issued to Mr. Roarke." Mr. Potter's tone reflected his distaste. As a corporate lawyer, he obviously felt that people's private lives should be handled more tidily. "Would you like me to contact him, Arianna? I could see that the proper steps are taken, straighten out this situation for you once and for all."

Arianna hesitated, her mind torn between the memories of love that had haunted her and the agony of rejection and betrayal that had followed so swiftly. She knew it would be easy to let Mr. Potter handle it. Then she could just finish packing her personal belongings and leave Denver behind. But she was no longer that frightened insecure girl, she realized; she had finally grown up, and grown-ups didn't run away.

"No, Mr. Potter, thank you, but this is something I have to handle myself. I'll be flying to Pellington Island to settle things, as soon as I can make the arrangements."

"Your father wouldn't approve of that, Arianna," Mr. Potter counseled. "This is a situation to be handled by an attorney, perhaps even more so now that things have gone so badly for you financially."

"Then I'd appreciate the names of some attorneys I can contact in the Seattle-Victoria area," Arianna answered. "Unless you would want to represent me in the proceedings."

His silence was a reproof. "I'll send over a list of names along with some papers that need your signature," he replied at last, his tone radiating disapproval. "There are things that must be taken care of before you can go off to Canada."

Arianna murmured proper assurances, but hung up the receiver determined to go ahead with this final confrontation. The firmness carried her onto the plane at Stapleton Airfield, sure that she had to take full charge of her own life even while doubts ate at the foundations of her courage.

Was she making a terrible mistake? Would she find more pain when she reached Pellington Island? What would happen when she saw Paul again? Memories swept over her in a breathtaking flood.

The storybook romance—walking hand in hand through the magnificent islands, the kisses stolen in spring-laden bowers, lovemaking on the deserted beaches, beneath friendly sun and even friendlier stars. And the days and nights on the beloved *Pelican*, waking in her husband's arms, learning to cook simple meals in the tiny, incredibly efficient galley—talking, dreaming, sharing.

How could it have been a sham? she asked herself as she had asked five years ago and a thousand times since. How could Paul have been pretending?

Yet if he had loved her, if he'd cared for her at all, why hadn't he come after her, fought for her? That had always been her father's single unassailable argument, and even now that he was dead, she couldn't refute it.

The war of memories and doubts continued through

the landing at Sea-Tac, the airport that served both Seattle and Tacoma, Washington, and haunted her through an uneasy night in a small hotel. She sat alone in her room, staring at the telephone, thinking of Joy, wondering if she should call her.

But the year in Europe with her father had broken their once close friendship. Right or wrong, Arianna had known that her father blamed Joy for what had happened, and when he'd insisted that she attend a different college, she hadn't fought him. A part of her hadn't wanted to face the questions she knew would be in Joy's eyes. They still exchanged newsy Christmas letters and Arianna knew of Joy's marriage and her new baby, but the closeness was gone.

Joy had been a part of the beginning of the happiest days of her life; she had no desire to force her to share what would be the final chapter of the saddest time. Perhaps she could contact her later, once she'd seen Paul and made peace with the unfinished hurt between them. She pushed all thoughts of the future away and went instead to the dining room to eat a solitary dinner, retiring early, since she'd already booked a seat on a late-morning seaplane that would take her to Pellington Island.

Things went smoothly the next day. The seaplane carried a dozen passengers bound for the various islands included on its itinerary. Arianna settled herself with a magazine, choosing a window seat so that she could effectively ignore the middle-aged man who sat beside her. It was not a time for talking to strangers.

Her mind was traveling back in time even more rapidly than the plane was moving through the cloud-drifted sky. For a moment she thought only of their triumphant honeymoon voyage, the final plans they'd made for shopping, and a special dinner at the Empress Hotel when they docked in Victoria. Plans that had been lost forever when the dream was shattered.

Paul left the *Pelican* shortly after they docked, kissing her with longing, then sighing and shaking his head. "You've got me ruined, woman," he told her. "I don't care where Mike has berthed the *Star* or whether or not he's managed to book another group. I don't even want to think about handling anything but my wife." His fingers trailed over her ribs.

"You'd better go before I haul you back to the cabin," she teased. "Just don't forget that I have to go shopping before our dinner tonight, unless you can get my clothes from the *Star*. I can't go to the Empress in the jeans I've been wearing."

"Or not wearing," was his parting quip as he left the boat.

Since years of discipline had made Paul extremely neat about the boat, there was little for her to do while she waited, so she used the time to make a list of the supplies they'd need. She was halfway through the list when she heard footsteps on deck.

"Hey, that didn't take long at all," she called, hurrying up to greet Paul with a kiss. When she reached the deck, however, she stopped dead, unable to believe her eyes.

"I've come for you, Arianna," her father said, his dark eyes burning with anger, though his voice was soft and controlled. "It is time for you to go home."

"Daddy!" It was the only word she could force past

the huge lump in her throat. When she caught her breath, she continued, "How . . . ?"

"Did you really think your telegram wouldn't bring me back home, Arianna?" he demanded. "Did you think I'd sit calmly in South America while you sailed around in some battered little boat with that no-good drifter?"

Outrage overrode her initial shock. "Paul's not a drifter, and this is his father's boat. Paul owns the *Pellington Star*. We'll be living on it most of the time while we take tours in the summer, then—"

"You will be living in Denver." His low voice cut through her words. "Get your things."

"I'm not going anywhere. This is my home and Paul is my husband." She forced herself to take a calming breath, a little frightened by the rage she could see building in her father's face. "I know you're angry, Daddy, and I'm sorry if you're angry because we got married so quickly, but once you have a chance to meet Paul—"

"We've met." The statement was flat.

"Then where is he?" Arianna asked. "Did he bring you to the boat? Why didn't he come aboard with you? How did you meet him, anyway? Did he know you were in Victoria?"

Her father snorted, then moved past her to drop on one of the benches in the upper cabin that was their living room and dining room. "He wouldn't have come to Victoria if he'd known I'd track him down so easily."

"But he went ashore to send you another telegram about our plans," Arianna protested. "I wanted you to meet him, to see how wonderful he is."

"Cut it out, baby," her father interrupted, his anger draining away and leaving what looked suspiciously like pity in his face. "Don't waste yourself on him, Arianna. He's not worth it. He's a two-bit opportunist who saw his big chance to marry money. He's not worth your tears, honey, believe me."

"No!" It had been part protest, part wail, but the single word echoed in the cabin, making her wince away from the sound. "You're wrong," she began, fighting for control. "When Paul comes, he'll tell you. He loves me and I love him. He's the most wonderful man in the world." But she couldn't go on when she saw the shattering compassion in her father's eyes. Under it she felt stripped naked and pitied.

"He isn't coming, Arianna, not today, not tomorrow. He married you because you're my daughter, my only child, my heir. He doesn't love you and he never did. I'm sorry to tell you that, but you have to realize it for your own good. He saw a chance to make a real life for himself and he grabbed it; he just didn't count on my seeing through him so quickly."

"You're wrong!"

"If I'm wrong, why did he agree to my terms so quickly? Why isn't he here beside you, defending this wonderful love that you're supposed to be sharing? Face it, honey, he seduced a young, innocent child and made you believe that it was love."

"I'll never believe that." She kept herself from screaming only by sheer effort of will. "I know Paul loves me, and when he comes back to the boat, he'll tell you that himself."

"How long do you propose to wait?"

The question was such an odd one that it broke through her pain and made her lift her eyes to her father's face once again. She tried to understand his meaning, but nothing truly made sense without Paul beside her.

"I'm asking you, Arianna," her father repeated, "how long will you wait for him to return before you'll be willing to believe that I've told you the truth?"

"I'll never believe it." She tried to make her voice firm and emphatic, but beneath the words even she could hear the first rising tide of doubt. It had happened so fast, this wonderful magic. One moment she'd been shy Arianna Kane trying to learn the secrets of love and flirting from Joy; then suddenly Paul had swept into her life and changed everything. He'd been in such a hurry—had it really only been because he loved her so much?

"I'd like to leave tonight," her father said, "but if you don't believe me, I'm willing to give him till morning to return to you."

"But we were going out to dinner," Arianna protested. "He went to make the reservations at the Empress; then we were going shopping so I'd have a dress."

Even as she spoke the words, she knew that it wasn't going to happen. Though she might tell herself that this was simply a bad dream, the proof that it wasn't was in her father's eyes.

"He's making reservations, all right," her father said, his tone bitter. "But they're for one and for out of town. He's going back where he came from now that I've paid him off. He's even planning to let someone else pick up this old tub."

"You did what?" Arianna gasped.

"I gave him what he wanted, honey. I paid him off to get him out of your life. It wasn't the amount he wanted, but when he found out I wasn't the fool he thought I was, he decided that it was enough."

"I don't believe you."

"Perhaps by tomorrow morning you will." His tone was gentle, but his gaze was implacable. "Shall I stay here, or will you come with me to a decent hotel?"

"I won't leave here till I see Paul." She said the words with as much determination as she could muster, but the doubt was already there. Where was Paul? If he'd met her father, why hadn't he come back here with him? Why had Paul left her all alone to face her father's anger?

"I'll go ashore and use the marina phone to call and have someone take care of my plane for the night, and I'll cancel my hotel reservation. I'll stay here until you're ready to face the truth."

Arianna just looked at him, wanting to argue and wanting to run, but not knowing what to say or where she could go to escape the pain that was boiling through her. Her father left her without a backward glance, his confidence doing even more to undermine her feelings.

Alone on the *Pelican*, Arianna paced. She wanted to see Paul, to beg him to tell her what was going on, but she had no idea where he was. Tears burned in her eyes, but she forced herself to look at her ring, to stare at the gleaming gold band and believe in it.

Paul wouldn't abandon her, she told herself. Her father might have said something to hurt him and make him stay away for a while, but once he had a chance to think, he'd be sure to realize that she was here and that she loved him.

For a moment fantasies of love filled her mind; then her attention was diverted by all that her father had said. He'd been so sure, and her father always seemed to be right. The warring thoughts tortured her as she paced and fussed about the boat, unable to sit down but with nothing to do and nowhere to go.

Footsteps on the deck brought a rise of hope, which was dashed immediately as her father stepped back into the cabin. He was carrying a battered overnight case. "Where do you want me to put this?"

"The guest cabin is that way," Arianna answered, feeling younger than before and more vulnerable. "You can sleep in there."

"What about food?" her father asked over his shoulder, not seeming to notice the lack of welcome in her voice.

"I'm afraid we don't have much on board," Arianna answered numbly. "Paul and I were going to get some provisions today." The mention of his name brought pain, but she endured it. "I can do some eggs for lunch. An omelet maybe, or just scrambled with ham on the side, if you prefer. Whatever."

"You won't let me take you somewhere in the city for a decent meal?" he asked.

Arianna shook her head. "I told you, I won't leave this boat until I've talked to Paul."

He sighed. "That's not going to happen, Arianna," he warned sadly. "I'm sorry, but it just won't work out that way. He hasn't the courage to face you with his shame."

The leaden silence spread between them till she could bear it no more. "How do you want your eggs?" she asked at last.

"Can you really make an omelet?" her father inquired, his tone mocking.

"Just be ready to eat it when I finish," Arianna told him, accepting his challenge.

Fixing the meal took some time, and it wasn't quite as perfect as she'd hoped, but it was good enough to offer to her father. Yet when she sat down at the table with him, she found that she couldn't swallow anything. Paul had taught her to make the omelet, just as he'd taught her to cook the fish they caught and to fix the other simple meals they'd shared.

"Don't think about it, Arianna," her father said, his voice soft and gentle with understanding. "I don't doubt that you love him. He's an attractive man, and with his years of experience, it would have taken a much older and wiser woman not to fall for his line."

"He loved me, too." Her voice cracked with doubt, and the final word was almost a sob.

"I'll see to it that you have an annulment. Make it so this marriage has never existed. It was a fraud, Arianna, and I'm sure I can prove it. You'll never have to see him again."

"But—"

He cut her off. "We'll go to Europe together, take a whole year if you like." He went on as though he hadn't heard her protest. "You'll forget him once you're away from here, and eventually the right man will come along. I'll help you find him, and when it happens, it will be as though this little mistake never happened."

"No, Daddy, no!" Her words were a sob. "I love Paul and he loves me. He won't let me go, you'll see." She got to her feet and left the table, unable to face him any longer. "There will never be anyone else!"

The afternoon was an eternity. She tried to hide in her room, but memories of Paul were hiding there, too.

She couldn't endure being where they'd made love so
often and so wonderfully. The deck and the other
cabins were little better, especially when she felt her
father's compassionate eyes following her.

For dinner her father again suggested they leave the
boat. When she refused to go with him, he ordered a
meal delivered, then insisted that she eat it.

The hours marched on, suddenly moving faster, slipping away too quickly. Each ticking minute was a weight,
for each minute separated her further from Paul, from
the hope that her father was wrong.

Late in the evening there were footsteps on the deck.
She burst out of the cabin with hope shining in her
eyes, but despair stopped her when she saw not Paul,
but Mike Jeffers.

"I brought your things, Arianna," he said with a wide
grin, setting the suitcase on the deck.

"Did Paul tell you to bring them?" Arianna asked,
hoping for some answers, a shred of hope to cling to.

"Paul?" Mike looked surprised at the question. "I
haven't seen him since the morning he took off after
you. Joy just asked me to hold the stuff after we got
your telegram." His grin deepened as he offered her
his good wishes.

"How did you know we were here?" Arianna asked,
holding back tears with fierce pride.

"Guy from one of the other boats mentioned that the
Pelican was in port, so I thought I'd make my delivery.
Is Paul aboard? I'd like a chance to congratulate him."

"I'm sorry, Mr. . . . ah . . ." Her father stepped out of
the cabin, saving her the pain of answering the question.
"Paul isn't here at the moment, but I do thank you for

bringing my daughter's belongings. You've saved us a trip tomorrow. May I pay you for your trouble?"

Arianna saw the anger and shock in Mike's face, felt the questions in his gaze, but she was beyond explanations. Mike's hasty exit left her feeling somehow more abandoned than she had felt before. Suddenly she didn't believe that Paul was coming back. The Paul she'd known and loved would have been here by now—if he'd ever existed.

Stubborn determination kept her wakeful and miserable in her bed through the night; but in the morning, disappointment, exhaustion, and despair allowed her to bend to her father's insistence that her husband was not coming back. She knew of no reason for Paul to be away so long, no reason why he wouldn't have contacted her.

"He must have your address in Denver," her father told her calmly. "We'll be there several days before we leave for Europe. Leave him a note if you like. I doubt that he'll abandon the boat for long. He'll probably come back for it, once he knows that we've gone." He smiled. "Or perhaps he'll have that man of his pick it up. In any case, he'll get the message, I'm sure."

He left her alone with a sheet of paper, but no matter how hard she tried to write, the words simply refused to flow. Her pain blocked her very thoughts. In the end, she left nothing behind but crumpled pages that looked just the way her heart felt.

She was no longer Arianna Kane Roarke, filled with love and pride and the magic of being alive. The person who followed Benton Kane off the *Pelican* was merely the husk. Her heart remained behind.

*   *   *

Arianna felt the warmth of fresh tears on her cheeks as her mind returned to the present. She kept her face turned to the window so that no one would see them. Paul had never come to find her, never written, never tried in any way to reach her. She'd believed her father's statement about the annulment because Paul had never shown any sign of concern for her. In time she'd even managed to convince herself that she didn't care.

But now all that was changed. Her father's insistence that Paul's lack of protest meant he'd freed her willingly in return for money made no sense to her. If Paul had never loved her, why hadn't he ended their marriage? Why was there no divorce?

Chapter Eight

❧

"Are you going to Pellington Island?" The voice was friendly but not demanding.

Arianna swallowed hard and took a deep breath. She'd dried her tears while they were landing at the last island, and now she almost welcomed the interruption.

"Yes, I am," she admitted, turning to look at the elderly gentleman who had taken the seat next to her after the other man left the plane. "Are you?"

"Been going there every summer for about twenty years," the man responded. "Name's Harvey Woodruff."

"Arianna Kane," Arianna said, then swallowed hard, realizing that her name was, as yet, a lie.

"Your first visit?" His pale blue eyes studied her shrewdly. "You don't look like a fisherman, though these days I find I'm less able to tell." His chuckle was easy.

Arianna felt herself blushing. "I'm not a fisherman," she admitted. "I was here once five years ago."

"Well, it is a beautiful spot, that's sure. But it's been changing for the last three years. Fact is, I hardly recognize the place anymore. The new hotel brings a lot of different people to the island." He sighed. "The fishing is still as good, but I guess I'm resenting the popularity because I liked it better the way it was."

"There's a new hotel?" Arianna felt a hollow growing in the pit of her stomach. "The fish camp is gone?" She couldn't say Paul's last name, but she knew that Mr. Woodruff would know what she meant.

Mr. Woodruff nodded his silvery head. "Ever since young Roarke took over the resort, it's been growing and changing. He says he's going to make it the most popular resort in the area, and I believe he will."

"Paul Roarke?" she asked as calmly as she could.

"Do you know him?" he asked.

"I did," Arianna answered. "But it was a long time ago."

"If it was more than four or five years ago, you won't recognize him," Mr. Woodruff informed her with a sigh. "He used to be a nice, easygoing guy. Had a fine charter boat and just enjoyed life. Before that he used to take out fishing parties for his father. Went out with him myself a few times. He seemed happy then, but since that time, his only drive has been to succeed in business."

"What happened to Mr. and Mrs. Roarke?" Arianna asked, remembering how friendly the couple had been. Had it been only because Paul had told them she was a potential heiress? She found that hard to believe.

"The mister had a bad fall on the ice winter before last, and they've pretty much turned things over to Paul. They have a home in Florida now. According to Paul, his father is building up a clientele for the fishing boat he has berthed down there." He smiled. "Did you know them?"

"Met them once briefly," Arianna answered.

"They're good folks. I hope they'll be coming to the hotel while I'm still chasing fish this summer."

Mr. Woodruff lapsed into silence. Arianna sighed. She had a thousand questions, but she knew she'd shown enough curiosity. She didn't want to have to explain her interest in people she'd claimed to have known only briefly. She was relieved when another passenger announced that they were passing an interesting island.

Though Arianna looked out the window obediently, she saw nothing except the past. If there had been any way to leave the plane and return to Seattle without the stop on Pellington Island, she would have taken it. She was suddenly sure that she wasn't strong enough or mature enough to face the past.

The seaplane, however, flew on serenely, and long before she was ready, she saw the familiar deep green, tree-covered bulk of Pellington Island. Love swept over her like the waves that washed the shore, and for just a moment she believed that she could make things right. Somewhere there must be a hope that her father had been wrong.

The seaplane settled into the cove flawlessly, bouncing over the water to the dock. Arianna searched the scene outside, hoping to see Paul waiting on the dock or to recognize his broad-shouldered form standing on the handsome deck that surrounded the startlingly white resort hotel that rose above the half-moon cove, dominating it as the old fishing camp never had.

"Time to get off, I guess," Mr. Woodruff murmured.

"It's been a pleasure talking to you and I hope we'll see each other at the hotel."

Too dry-mouthed to answer, Arianna forced a smile as she gathered her hand luggage and moved down the aisle toward the door, following Mr. Woodruff's sturdy form. The day, golden and promising when they'd left Seattle, had dimmed to threatening, and the air that touched her burning cheeks was wet with the expectation of rain. Arianna shivered, remembering another rainy night.

"Mr. Woodruff . . . Mr. and Mrs. Harper, welcome to Pellington Island Resort."

The feminine voice stopped Arianna in her tracks. She looked around for Paul, memory having made her hope again. If they couldn't find the past, she suddenly thought, there was still the future. If there had been even a little love on his part, wasn't there just a chance . . . ?

Paul was nowhere to be seen, but a tall red-haired woman was staring at her curiously. Arianna took a deep breath and managed a weak smile.

"Excuse me," the redhead said, her hazel eyes puzzled despite her professional welcoming smile. "Are we expecting you, miss?"

Arianna started to answer, but the dilemma of her name kept her from speaking. After a moment, she simply shook her head.

"You must be the girl from the Hannigan Agency," the redhead guessed, her expression changing slightly. "If you'll just wait in the lobby until I get the guests settled, we'll talk about the job." She returned her attention to the guests. "This way, folks."

Arianna found herself standing alone as the redhead shepherded the guests along the dock and a young

man in a forest-green uniform followed them with the
small wagon of luggage that had been unloaded from
the plane. She took several steps after them, then
hesitated, aware that she could still change her mind
and leave all this to Mr. Potter.

But could she? Would she ever be able to forget Paul
if she didn't see him face to face? Five years hadn't
banished the joy or the pain; five more might not either.
As she watched, the seaplane door closed and the moor-
ing lines dropped. The motors flared to life and the
plane was on its way.

Feeling conspicuous in her elegant pantsuit, Arianna
moved along the dock in the wake of the luggage cart,
feeling just a little like she was stepping into one of her
own long-ago fantasies. At any moment she expected
the doors of the resort to open and Paul to step out to
greet his guests—and to see her. However, when the
doors finally did open for the entourage, there was
only another dark-green-clad young man, who'd come
to help with the mound of luggage.

Arianna followed everyone into the lobby, then
stopped, her breath catching in her throat. The white-
painted exterior had made her expect a modern room,
but this looked more like the old fishing camp.

Soft, slightly shabby furniture was grouped for conversation in several areas of the big room, including
one pair of love seats that seemed to be warming them-
selves before a huge smoke-touched stone fireplace.
Though no fire burned on the hearth, Arianna crossed
the well-polished hardwood floor to sit on the nearest
of the love seats.

What was she going to do? she asked herself. How
could she face Paul? It had seemed so essential before,

but now that she was here and he might simply stride into the room, all her doubts about her own appeal returned. She might be older and a little wiser, but if he didn't love her, was she any more able to bear the rejection?

"Ah, there you are." It was the redhead coming down the stairway that gave access to the rooms on the second and third floors of the resort. "I'm Leila Humbolt, and you are . . . ?"

"Arianna Kane," Arianna answered, deciding that she'd use the name she was sure was hers—using "Roarke" could wait till after she'd seen Paul. She tried to find words of explanation, but Leila Humbolt appeared to be only half-listening to her name and was already going on.

"The agency didn't call me, I'm afraid, so I have no idea of your qualifications, Miss Kane," the redhead stated, a quizzical expression in her eyes. "However, if you can type, talk to people, and hand out keys, you have a job. With Paul away for a week, I'm going crazy. My desk clerk broke his hip in a boating accident yesterday morning and this place is really going to be busy for the next few days. We're booked full starting with the weekend."

Arianna didn't absorb too much of what Leila Humbolt was saying, but the words about Paul filled her mind with alternating waves of relief and disappointment. She'd been braced for the confrontation, and now it seemed she'd been granted a reprieve.

"Well, what do you say?" Leila asked, tucking in a stray strand of her sleekly coiled hair. "Are you going to stay and help me out, Miss Kane?"

Arianna looked around, trying to make a decision. If

the resort was booked full, she couldn't simply ask for a room. Miss Humbolt was handing her the perfect solution to her problem. Staying here as an employee would give her an ideal way to find out all about Paul and what had happened to him since the morning he'd kissed her a loving good-bye and disappeared out of her life.

"I'll give the job a try," she told the expectant and slightly impatient-looking redhead. "What exactly did you want me to do?"

"You do type?"

Arianna nodded. "I'm not exactly speedy, but I am accurate."

"Then you can start by typing the menus for tonight. I'm hopeless with a typewriter." Leila laughed. "Paul says when I sit down at the typewriter, someone moves the keys."

Arianna's laugh was polite, but she felt a pang at the woman's casual way of talking about Paul. Suddenly frightened, she looked at Leila's elegant hands. She wore several rings, but the delicate flower design of the one on her left hand didn't look like either an engagement or a wedding ring.

"I know you must be anxious to see your room and get your things unpacked," Leila continued, "but if you'll type up the menus for dinner first, I can get one of the boys to run them off so we can use them tonight. Would you mind?"

"Whatever you say, Miss Humbolt," Arianna replied, studying the woman from under her thick golden-brown lashes. Her curiosity was fully aroused now that her fear of meeting Paul was allayed.

" 'Leila,' please, Arianna," the redhead corrected, her

eyes appraising but unreadable. "We aren't that formal here on Pellington."

"Leila," Arianna agreed, uncomfortable now with the attractive woman. Where did she fit into Paul's life? Was she the reason he'd never tried to contact her? Had she been here waiting for him when he returned with Benton Kane's money to make his dream of a resort come true?

Arianna swallowed hard, pushing the suspicions away, forcing herself to pay attention to what Leila was telling her about the menus as they crossed the lobby to the hotel office. Under other circumstances, she had the feeling that she might like this woman, who seemed so confident and competent.

Once Arianna was settled at the typewriter, Leila bustled out of the small office, leaving her alone. She began to type at once, grateful for all the practice she'd had in her years at college. Though she'd made good grades and finished very high in her graduating class, Arianna had a strong suspicion that her liberal-arts courses had done little to prepare her for finding the kind of job that she would soon need. Her trust fund was generous, but not enough for her to live on the rest of her life. It was nice to know that she had one useful skill, she thought with a wry smile. After all, she would be seriously seeking a job once this final bit of her past was settled. In resort work? It was no more unreal than the position she now found herself in.

Thoughts of her uncertain future sobered her completely and she concentrated on the menu, copying the final lines from an old menu that Leila had given her as a sample. It was such a simple job, she wondered if Leila had asked her to do it as a test of her skills.

Leila returned just as Arianna was taking the stencil from the typewriter, giving credence to her suspicion. She scanned it quickly, then smiled. "Terrific. One problem solved, anyway." Her smile seemed a bit more natural now. "Would you like to see your room? I'm sure you'd like a little time to relax before you have to get ready for dinner. And I should show you around the resort a bit, too, I suppose."

"I'd love to see it," Arianna agreed. "It is very beautiful."

"We're proud of it," Leila answered, her voice warm.

"Sounds like you've been here for quite a while," Arianna observed, purposely focusing her attention on covering the typewriter and gathering up her purse and tote bag, which she'd placed beside the desk.

"Ever since we opened the resort," was Leila's disturbing answer.

"How long ago was that?" Arianna forced herself to ask, suddenly sure that she wasn't going to like the answer.

"We celebrated four years in May." Leila's eyes softened. "Of course, it wasn't like this back then. There were just four guest cabins, and the whole main building would have fit in our lobby, with room to spare." She looked around with an air of ownership that sent a chill down Arianna's spine. "It had been a fishing camp, so it wasn't easy to change the image at first."

"It's certainly far more than that now," Arianna managed, her heart aching at the memories Leila's words had evoked.

"Once Paul decided what he wanted to do, it didn't take him long to make things happen." Leila laughed. "Now, come along and I'll give you a quick tour before

I show you to your room. And of course, you'll want the details about your job, won't you?" There was a note of something else in the woman's voice, but Arianna couldn't place it. Mockery, perhaps?

She tried to study Leila, but found her face singularly hard to read. She was obviously a complex person, but Arianna could tell little beyond that at the moment.

The whirlwind tour Leila gave Arianna left her slightly confused, but impressed. The resort was as handsome as any her father had taken her to and seemed well-staffed and efficiently run. The large dining room, which shared the first floor with the lobby, kitchen, office, and staff quarters, was already being prepared for dinner and the scents that came from the dazzlingly efficient kitchen set her stomach to rumbling. Arianna was reminded that she'd had no appetite for lunch.

She was relieved when Leila opened one of the doors that lined the corridor behind the office. "I hope you'll be comfortable here, Arianna," she said. "I had the boys put your luggage on the rack. The bath is through there, and if you need anything, I'll be somewhere in the lobby area. There's another party due in sometime this evening. They're coming by boat, so they may not get in before dark."

Curiosity prompted Arianna to smile and say, "Goodness, your boss must have great confidence in you to be gone for so long during such a busy time."

"My boss?" Leila frowned. "Oh, you mean Paul? He's not my boss, Arianna, he's my partner and my very dear friend." Her tone underlined the "very" just a little.

A bell sounded from the front desk, and Leila was gone before Arianna could find her voice or take con-

trol of the emotions that suddenly seemed to whirl
through her. She sank down on the flowered bedspread and stared at the door that Leila had closed
behind her.

It didn't take a genius to figure out what "very dear
friend" meant. Leila Humbolt was a beautiful, sophisticated woman, precisely the type that she'd thought
Paul would prefer.

The pain stabbed bitterly, yet she knew that now, five
years later, she had no right to be jealous. Mr. Potter
had been right: coming here was a terrible mistake.
Just talking to Paul, learning the answers to the questions that had tormented her, wouldn't make any
difference. Those questions were five years out of date.

The past was past—that was what she had to accept.
Confirming her father's story would prove nothing,
disproving it even less. Paul was not a man to be without a woman; the power and delicious variety of his
lovemaking had told her that. It was plain that he'd
moved on from the girl he'd seduced and left; she'd
been a sentimental fool to think that she could claim his
love now.

But what of the still-standing marriage? That wasn't
a question in the past, not if it existed today. Weary
beyond her twenty-three years, she pulled her shattered courage over her confused thoughts, then unpacked the soft print dress that she would wear to
dinner. It was too late to escape the island tonight, she
was sure. But tomorrow she would simply tell Leila that
she couldn't stay; someone else could ask the questions.

Fortified by her decision, she spent some time smooth-
ing her hair into elegant waves that fell softly to her
shoulders, then touched makeup to the lashes of her

brown eyes. It was suddenly very important that no one should guess that she was anything but a new temporary employee.

By the time Arianna made her way through the rear hall and office out to the lobby, the earlier storm had cleared, making room for a truly spectacular sunset. Though it was still half an hour before dinner was to be served, Mr. Woodruff was in the lobby. He rose from one of the soft chairs the moment she entered the big room.

"Ah, Miss Kane, I was hoping you'd be coming out early," he greeted her. "It's going to be a nice evening for us, after all."

Arianna smiled, finding the old gentleman a welcome diversion. "I'm afraid I was so busy I didn't even notice the storm." She went on to explain that she was temporarily working for the resort.

"If you're free, would you like to take a turn around the deck with me?" he asked, accepting her words without surprise or comment. "We could watch the clouds changing color now that sunset is near. This is the best time of day, don't you think? Almost a shame to waste it eating dinner."

Arianna smiled. "Depends on how hungry you are," she replied. "I've been smelling dinner cooking for an hour, and I have to admit that I'm about to starve."

"Do you have plans for dinner?" Mr. Woodruff asked. "Or are you free to keep an old gentleman company on his first night here?"

"I'd be delighted to have your company," Arianna told him, meaning it. Having spent so many years as her father's hostess, she was generally quite comfortable in the company of older people, and Mr. Woodruff was a very charming man.

They circled the huge building twice, following the deck all the way around and enjoying the changing vistas that each side offered. The deep green of the forest behind the building and the neatly manicured lawn that spread between the main lodge and the small cabins that still stood on each side were charming, but the best view was the beautiful shoreline in front. Arianna stared at the curved arms of the island that extended out to embrace the water of the cove and wondered how it would have been if her father hadn't found them that morning in Victoria.

Would they have entered the cove in the *Pelican*? What kind of welcome would have been waiting? What sort of husband would Paul have been if her father hadn't come between them? She swallowed hard, realizing at last that this was what she'd come to Pellington Island to find out.

"You're very quiet," Mr. Woodruff observed.

"I was just thinking how beautiful it is here," Arianna said.

"I liked it better before," Mr. Woodruff stated firmly. "Place like this is too much to handle. When Paul's father was here, it was all so simple and easy."

"It's lucky for Paul that he has Leila to manage things for him when he's away," Arianna observed, wondering how much Mr. Woodruff could tell her about Paul and Leila's relationship.

"I don't suppose he could have done it without her," Mr. Woodruff admitted. "And he really needed help after his father had that bad fall. Of course, Miss Humbolt was with him from the beginning."

"He must have invested a fortune in the place," Arianna continued, her fingers nervously caressing the pine railing of the deck, while she willed Mr. Woodruff to tell her that the money was Leila's and not the price of Paul's love.

"That's for sure. Never did hear where the money came from, either. One year I came and it was the old fishing camp, the next year when I came back, they'd torn down the old house and were building the resort. Paul was taking out parties night and day—a man possessed, and not just with his dream of building the resort, either. He was a different person." He shrugged. "I never did know what changed him."

Arianna closed her eyes. She knew what had changed him, and now she was quite sure she knew where he'd found the money that had built the resort. Her father's payoff must have been higher than she'd ever guessed.

"But I shouldn't be boring you with ancient history about someone you hardly know," Mr. Woodruff said, taking her arm. "If I remember correctly, you told me that you were starving, and I believe they just opened the dining room for dinner."

For a moment she stood still, not acknowledging his touch, the lump of pain filling her throat so that she was sure she'd never be able to swallow a bite. But slowly her anger returned to ease the hurt and lift her golden head. Her smile was far from genuine, and the sparkle in her eyes came from unshed tears, but Mr. Woodruff didn't seem to notice.

"Lead me to the food," she told him.

Dinner was interminable. Leila joined them, flirting charmingly with Mr. Woodruff while telling them a few stories about the beginning of the resort and the struggle that she and Paul had had. It did nothing to ease Arianna's feeling that Leila and Paul were meant for each other. By dessert she didn't even need to exaggerate when she told them that she had a headache. She asked to be excused, and fled to the sanctuary of her room.

She was tired, but once she'd changed into her plainest pair of satin pajamas, she found herself unable to settle down to rest. Confused and miserable, she wandered to the window. It was open to admit the damp scents of the night, and as she looked across the grass, she could see the lights still burning in two of the old cabins.

Paul had helped build those cabins when he was a boy, she thought sadly. She remembered so much of what he'd told her about this place and about his dreams and plans for it. She'd wanted to share those dreams with him, help him create them, but instead he'd taken what her father had offered him. A payoff to let her go! This place was the result of her father's payoff—that seemed to be the only thing that made sense.

Yet what of the marriage? Had Paul cheated her father by not going through with the divorce he'd undoubtedly promised to get? And why? With Leila here waiting to marry him, why would he have kept their marriage legal?

It always came back to that, she realized, retreating to her bed and placing her aching head on the pillow. Could she unravel the jigsaw puzzle of the past by staying here? She slept abruptly without having found an answer, and woke feeling even more depressed.

Arianna was trying to subdue the wild curls that the damp air had brought to her hair when a knock on her door interrupted. "Arianna, are you awake?" Leila demanded.

Arianna gave up on her hair and opened the door. "I'm sorry," she said. "Was I supposed to be in the office this early?" She looked at her travel alarm, which showed that it was only a little after seven.

Leila shook her head, looking guilty. "Oh, no, it's not that," she admitted. "In fact, I have to apologize for interrupting you so early, but we have another crisis."

"Crisis?" Arianna echoed the word dubiously, sensing that what Leila said next might very well upset her plan to invent an excuse to leave the island today.

"I'm afraid you're going to have to take over for me for the day," Leila continued. "I know it's unfair, since you haven't had time to learn the ropes, but we have a scheduled trip into Victoria for the guests today. I don't usually act as hostess and guide, but since Paul is gone and Preston is laid up, we don't have much choice." She sighed dramatically. "You won't have any trouble, I'm sure. Mr. Woodruff is already out in one of the small boats and won't be back till evening, and Mr. and Mrs. Coventry are the only other guests who won't be going on the *Star* with us."

Arianna started to protest that she wasn't a trained secretary or receptionist, but the mention of the *Star* froze the words in her throat.

"There's really nothing much to do," Leila continued, taking her silence for agreement. "Just answer the phone, take reservations—I'll show you the forms. You can make sure that the Coventrys are fed at noon and that the dinner menu is typed and run off before we get back."

Arianna met the redhead's worried gaze for another

few heartbeats, then mentally shrugged her shoulders. Paul was gone for a week, she reminded herself; another day here wouldn't make any difference, and it was obvious that Leila really did need help "Show me the reservation forms," she said. "I wouldn't want to over-book or anything like that."

"Bless you," Leila gasped, surprising her with a sudden friendly hug. "I just knew that you'd prove to be a great help. There is some other typing you might do if you get bored. I left it stacked by the typewriter. Of course, I don't expect you to get it all done today, but I know how much faster time passes when you're busy." They entered the desk-office area. "Now, these are the forms and this is the master register for the next three months," she explained.

The system was not complicated and the typing proved to be mostly forms or bills, which were easy enough to understand. By the time Leila had sorted out the chaos of getting the guests fed and onto the hauntingly familiar boat that was now tied up at the dock, Arianna was feeling able to handle everything for the day.

It was only when the boat sailed, leaving silence behind, that she felt the depression returning. Alone, she had to face the fact that she was playing a charade, and she could see no way that it could end happily.

Chapter Nine

The morning dragged by. The phone rang frequently enough to keep her from accomplishing a great deal at the typewriter. Toward noon the Coventrys came by to tell her that they wouldn't be at the resort for lunch since they were going to walk to the village to look in the island shops and have lunch at the Pellington Grotto, the island's restaurant.

"You'll have to try it yourself," Mrs. Coventry told Arianna with a smile. "They specialize in fresh fish. Whatever they catch in the morning is the special of the day, and their cook is wonderfully inventive." She paused, then added, "Not that the food here isn't super. It's just that the Grotto is different."

"I would like to see the village," Arianna admitted, wondering how much the quiet island settlement had been changed by the building of the larger resort.

"We'd ask you to go with us," Mr. Coventry said, "but I don't suppose you can leave the desk with Miss Humbolt gone."

"No, I have to stay close and answer the telephone,"

Arianna agreed, then laughed as the phone began to shrill right on cue.

"We'll see you later," Mrs. Coventry called over her shoulder as they headed for the door.

"Pellington Island Resort," Arianna answered in her most professional tone.

"Miss Humbolt?" The voice was male and none too friendly.

"I'm sorry, but she's not here right now," Arianna answered. "May I help you?"

"Can you cancel a reservation?"

"Why, yes, I guess so." Arianna was surprised. "If you'll give me your name and the dates involved, I'll make a note of it and Miss Humbolt can make the arrangements."

"The name is Dryer and the reservation is for next weekend."

Arianna shuffled through the papers, seeking the register, and then scanned the neat lines for his name. She couldn't find it anyplace. "This next weekend?" she asked, wondering if she could have misunderstood.

"Friday, Saturday, and Sunday nights." His voice was impatient as he added the dates.

"Well, Mr. Dryer, I don't seem to find any record of your having a reservation," Arianna admitted, feeling that she was handling the situation poorly, but not sure what else she could do. "Could it possibly have been booked under another name?"

"Why would it be? I don't have another name." His sarcasm was tangible.

"I realize that, but this is my first day here and I really don't know anything about past reservations. Perhaps there was an error."

"I have a letter of confirmation," Mr. Dryer stated coldly. "The name seems to be correct on it."

"Does the confirmation have the room number?" Arianna asked.

"Cabin four."

"Oh, you reserved a cabin," Arianna said, relieved. "I think that register is separate. Just a moment, let me—"

"Listen, whoever you are, just cancel the reservation for cabin four and have Miss Humbolt return my deposit when she gets back, all right?"

"I'll tell her, Mr. Dryer," Arianna answered, "and I'm sorry that I didn't understand that it was—"

The click stopped her apology. Arianna sighed and replaced the receiver. "Grouch," she told it. "I'm glad you can't come. Who needs someone like you around?"

Feeling put upon, she began opening the drawers that lined the back of the tall front desk, searching for a cabin register. She'd already made a note about the cancellation for Leila, but if someone else should call about renting a cabin, she wanted to have the most current information ready so she could answer their questions.

The drawers yielded a number of bits of information and registers of various types—boat rentals, equipment rentals, even charges for various services—but nothing about the cabins. She was about to give up hope when she spotted a manila file in the back of the bottom drawer.

"Boy, you sure know how to hide things, Leila," she muttered as she lifted the file out and opened the cover, sure that she'd finally found what she was seeking. Her eyes widened. Her father's face stared up at her from a rather poor newspaper picture. In the corner of the large photo was a small inset picture of her.

Arianna gasped, recognizing both photographs. The legend beneath the pictures stated that the photograph was of Benton Kane, the smaller one that of his daughter—the picture of her had been taken at his funeral. Her hand shook as she shifted that clipping to one side and stared at the newspaper clipping beneath it. It was unfamiliar, an attached card identifying it as having come from a financial paper several weeks before her father's death. Sick and confused, Arianna sorted through the thick bundle of papers, all the efficient work of a clipping service and all concerning the life and times of Benton Kane. The very bottom clipping, aged and dry, was over four years old. It was a lengthy Sunday-supplement article on the European tour that she and her father had taken.

Arianna closed the file slowly, shaken. What did it mean? It was another piece in the puzzle of her past, but like the others she'd found, it didn't seem to fit with any other piece.

As the first shock waves receded, another face came into her mind. Leila! Had the redhead seen the clippings? It seemed impossible that she could have missed them. And the newspaper photograph, though of poor quality, was recognizable. Also, now that she thought about it, she realized that Arianna Kane wasn't exactly a common name. She blushed to remember how casually she'd announced it, how naively she'd believed that she was unknown here. Then she frowned as her thoughts followed a logical course.

If Leila had recognized her, why the pretense? She might actually have been expecting a girl from the agency, but once she'd heard her name and taken a good look at her, she must have realized. Leila's act made no more sense than the other pieces of the puzzle.

Arianna replaced the file as she'd found it. She shook her head, wondering at the friendliness she'd felt from Leila, her own warming toward the woman during their brief acquaintance.

She clenched her teeth. When the group came back tonight, she'd face Leila with the file, she decided. She'd demand some answers, and then, perhaps, things might begin to make sense for her.

Time inched along. Since there were no guests to be fed, Arianna took her meal in the kitchen, using the time to get better acquainted with Flo, the single waitress on duty, and Charles, the taciturn middle-aged chef. The food was excellent, but it did nothing to fill the hollow inside her.

There were fewer calls in the afternoon, and she was glad when the Coventrys came in about two, looking content and well-satisfied. They paused at the desk as they had earlier.

"Been busy?" Mrs. Coventry asked.

"Not really," Arianna admitted. "Did you have a nice time in the village?"

"Oh, it was lovely," Mrs. Coventry gushed. "I would have liked to stay longer, but my husband thought we should come back."

"I think there's a storm coming," Mr. Coventry said. "No clouds yet, but there's something in the breeze."

His wife shook her head, smiling indulgently. "He always forecasts storms and all we have is sunshine." Her tone was full of laughter. "Sometimes I think he expects bad weather just because there are shops that I want to investigate."

Mr. Coventry chuckled. "Well, at least we're back in time for a nap before dinner."

"Oh, how can you even mention dinner after all we had to eat in the village?" Mrs. Coventry teased; then the two of them retreated to the stairway with friendly waves. Arianna watched them go with a pang of envious longing.

Was that the way it would have been for her and Paul? Would they have built up a lot of little jokes and teasing ways? Would their love have matured into something deep and gentle and special? She wanted to believe that it would, but she couldn't know if there had ever been any love from Paul. She prowled the lobby, too filled with nervous energy to settle quickly behind the desk or at the typewriter. Everywhere she looked, she saw Paul's image. She could picture him sitting on one of the love seats before a roaring fire or standing at the wide window staring out at the cove.

She followed her thoughts to the window and stood there, watching the water as it lapped on the rocks and set the small motorboats to bobbing beside the dock. The deep green of the pines was a stark contrast to the blue water. Even as she watched, the wind seemed to stir and begin to comb through the pine boughs. It was several seconds before she realized that the sky, which had been a blinding blue earlier, was now turning gray as clouds climbed from the horizon to obscure the sun. Arianna frowned at the clouds, then giggled, thinking that this time, at least, Mr. Coventry's forecast had been correct.

The ringing of the phone summoned her back to the

desk and she forced herself to sound enthusiastic as she said, "Pellington Island Resort."

"Arianna, this is Leila."

"Oh, hello." Arianna did her best to keep a quick rush of anger from showing in her voice.

"How is it going?" Leila asked.

"Pretty quiet," Arianna responded. "I've taken a couple of reservations, and a Mr. Dryer called to cancel his reservation for cabin four. I couldn't find the cabin register, but I figured you could handle it when you get back." Arianna paused. "Is there something else I should be doing?" she asked, suddenly realizing that there must be a reason for Leila's call.

"Well, actually, we've run into sort of a problem here, Arianna," Leila began, her tentative tone surprising Arianna.

"What's happened?"

"Mike just checked with the Weather Service and there's a serious squall forecast for the area around Pellington Island. They're warning all small craft to take shelter, so Mike doesn't think we should risk making the run back to the resort tonight."

"You're not coming back tonight?" Arianna gasped.

"It's inconvenient and expensive, but we can't risk taking all our guests through a storm, so we're just going to stay in Victoria till morning. We'll be out early, of course. I'm calling so you can tell the chef and so that you won't worry about us." She paused, then added, "You can handle everything there, can't you?"

"With just three guests, I think I can manage," Arianna replied. "What about new arrivals? Is anyone expected?"

"Not with this storm."

"Well, don't worry about anything," Arianna told

her. "We'll manage fine here. In fact, I expect Mr. Coventry will be pleased with the storm—he predicted it earlier today."

"He . . . Oh, well, fine." Leila sounded confused and harried. "We'll see you tomorrow then. Good-bye."

The line went dead and Arianna glared at the phone for a moment, resenting the call and the fact that she was trapped on the island, yet at the same time glad that Leila wouldn't be returning now. She needed more time to plan for their confrontation.

Mindful of Leila's instructions, Arianna went to the kitchen to inform the staff of the change in plans, agreeing with Charles that he and Flo could handle dinner. With that in mind, she sent the remaining staff home to their families on the other side of the island.

She tried typing for a while, but the windows seemed to call her, and she spent much of her time standing and watching the cove. The day continued to darken and the small boats no longer rocked gently near the dock. The wind whipped the waves to frothy white and the boats were bounced against the dock almost violently.

Arianna was typing when she heard the sound of a motor. At first she didn't give it a great deal of thought, but as the droning grew louder, she hurried to the window, suddenly hoping that it was the *Star* returning in spite of Leila's call.

The green-and-blue-striped helicopter was bucking and shaking as the winds tried to keep the white pontoons from touching the waves. The pilot, however, was up to the test and brought it to the water firmly, settling at just the right spot to be carried against the dock. Two men leaped out and began securing the helicopter to the dock. Arianna started to the door, but before she reached it, the phone shrilled a summons that she couldn't ignore. Sighing and grinding her teeth in frustration, she ran back to the desk and answered it. The call was a reservation and the details seemed interminable. By the time she'd taken all the information and was free to return, there was only one person on the dock. Arianna frowned, peering out as rain began to fall heavily.

The door opened and a figure stepped inside. Arianna turned around, opening her mouth to issue a welcome, but no words came out as her wide brown eyes met Paul's startled green ones. For what seemed an eternity there was only the sound of the rain and the wind whipping it against the windows; then Paul let his breath out slowly.

"What the hell are you doing here?" he demanded. "Couldn't you wait for your attorney to file for the divorce?"

"Paul . . . ?"

"Well, if you've come to make sure I agree to the divorce, you can rest assured that I won't fight you. All you ever had to do was ask."

"That's very kind of you," Arianna managed, hurt and anger killing the desperate longing she'd felt the moment she saw him.

"I've already assured your lawyer of that," he continued, his eyes suddenly evading hers.

"You what?"

"Did you really think I wouldn't know that your father was dead, Arianna? As soon as the news came out, I knew that I had to see you again. I went to Colorado, so I was a little surprised when your lawyer informed me that you were on your way north to discuss a divorce." He glanced at her, then looked away. "He didn't tell me that you'd planned to move in."

The viciousness of the words cut across her already lacerated nerves. "I'd be happy to leave," she announced, "but your partner asked me to mind the desk for her while she took your guests to Victoria for the day. The storm trapped them there." She stopped as the door opened again and a man came dashing in, dripping and gasping.

"Paul, you could drown a duck out there. I just hope you don't have any stray guests wandering around in this. Did you check with Leila? If . . ." He stopped, his eyes finally registering the fact that Arianna was there.

For a moment she just looked at the two men, not sure what to say; then a sudden image filled her mind. "Mr. Woodruff!" she gasped. "He hasn't come back from fishing."

The silence was heavy; then Paul sighed. "Sorry, David," he said. "Looks like we're going to be taking the chopper back out, unless Charles has heard something about Woodruff on the radio."

"Woodruff?" David asked.

"A seventy-year-old fisherman. He's liable to be pretty far out, and it's going to be a long cold night. I'll make a radio check."

"It's a good thing I started with a full tank," David observed. "Get some extra rain gear, Paul. And how about a couple of thermoses of coffee?" David looked toward Arianna.

"I'll get the coffee," Arianna replied, suddenly eager to escape Paul's unreadable eyes. She met Flo in the corridor and explained about Paul's arrival and Mr.

Woodruff, then gave her the order for the thermoses of coffee.

"I'll put together some sandwiches, too," Flo said with a sigh. "You can bet those two haven't eaten, and it could be a long night."

"Is there anything I can do to help?" Arianna asked.

Flo shook her head. "Not much anyone can do at a time like this. David is the best there is at search and rescue from the air, and Paul is tops on the water. I just hope Mr. Woodruff saw the storm coming and took shelter somewhere. It's going to get worse out there before it gets better."

Arianna stayed in the corridor, filled with uncertainty after Flo disappeared in the direction of the kitchen. Worry about Mr. Woodruff and his would-be rescuers warred with her hurt at Paul's treatment. He'd been so angry and cold.

Suddenly the truth dawned on her, striking like a blow to the stomach, and she fled into her room. He'd gone to Denver, all right, but not to get a divorce. He'd gone to claim his wife—Benton Kane's heir! Only he'd learned the truth about her inheritance; that was why he was so angry and cruel and eager for his freedom.

Sobs shook her body, so that she could do nothing but collapse on her bed. It was the first betrayal all over again, only this time she'd seen his face, heard the cold words from his lips. It didn't make her feel any better when she realized that she'd brought it on herself by coming here.

Her sobs lasted till she heard the thudding heartbeat of the helicopter blades as the men took off. The sound brought her off the bed to the window, but she could see little beyond the rail of the deck, for night had arrived prematurely. Feeling spent and beaten, she bathed her face, then dragged herself back to the desk in time to answer the phone.

Mr. and Mrs. Coventry came down as she was hanging up the receiver. "Did we hear a helicopter?" Mr. Coventry asked, coming over to the desk.

Arianna explained about Paul's brief return and immediate departure to search for Mr. Woodruff.

"Isn't this terribly dangerous weather for them to be flying?" Mrs. Coventry asked, looking toward the window.

"It seems to me that it would be," Mr. Coventry agreed. "I'm surprised that the pilot would take off before the end of the storm."

"David Hennessey would take off into a hurricane if there was someone to be rescued," Flo answered from the archway that connected lobby and dining room, "and Paul would go with him."

"Is it very dangerous?" Arianna asked, some of her anger fading at the thought.

Flo nodded, her face telling more than any words could. "Would you folks be wanting dinner early?" she asked.

"Whenever is best for you," Mrs. Coventry answered. "And just something simple, Flo. You must be anxious to get home to your family, too."

Flo smiled at the woman. "I don't worry too much. We've weathered a lot of storms on this island. I just hope that poor Mr. Woodruff is safe. He's always been secretive about where he likes to fish. He could be hard to find."

Silence followed that statement for several minutes; then Arianna became aware that Flo was looking at her expectantly. "What time would you like me to serve dinner, Arianna?" she asked at last.

Arianna swallowed hard, her fear taking any appetite that might have remained after her bout of tears. "Whenever is convenient," she answered, going to the window to stare out at nothing.

"About an hour, then," Flo said. "I'll monitor the weather reports and keep you informed, too."

The next hour dragged by even with the Coventrys for company. Flo continued to report on the weather, also bringing them the news that the phone lines on the island were down and that the shortwave radio was not working well. Even though the food was excellent, Arianna found it tasted like sawdust.

When Flo came in to serve their after-dinner coffee, Arianna stopped her to ask, "Shouldn't they be coming back soon, Flo? I mean, how long can that helicopter fly without refueling?"

Flo's eyes met hers squarely for a moment, then dropped. "Not this long," was her only answer.

Arianna pressed on. "Did he say anything about what they were going to do, Flo? Where they might go to look? I mean, shouldn't we be calling someone to report them missing?"

"All Paul said was to tell you that he wasn't going to let you off this island without an explanation—about everything." Flo's eyes suddenly reflected her curiosity. "Did you know him before, Arianna?"

She hesitated, ready to lie; then she remembered the file. Did everyone know about her childish attempt to pose as something she wasn't? In the face of Paul's danger, it seemed less important. "A long time ago," she replied. "Now, what about getting some help for them?"

"I'll talk to Charles, but I don't think we're going to be able to signal anybody with the resort radio. Charles has been working on it most of the afternoon, but it keeps getting worse." Flo sighed. "Anyway, David will have kept in radio contact with anyone who was listening. He's real experienced at search and rescue."

Arianna sought through her mind for something else she could suggest, something—anything—to help Paul, but there was nothing. Fear and frustration nearly choked her, but she forced herself to banish her private hell and continue her conversation with the Coventrys. She was relieved when they finally said good night and climbed the stairs to their room.

Arianna went immediately to the kitchen. Flo and Charles were just finishing their preparations for morning, and Charles turned to her with a sigh. "Will you be needing us here any longer, Arianna?" he asked.

"What about the radio, calling for help?" Arianna asked.

"No way. With patience, you can pick up an occasional weather report, but that's about it," Charles answered. "I've been warning Paul that it was on its last legs, but radios always go out when you need them, not when there's a repairman around." He shook his head as he went to get his and Flo's rain gear from the storage room beyond the kitchen. "We'll be in early in the morning," he said.

"You have a long wet walk ahead of you," Arianna observed.

"We're used to it," Flo answered, then added, "Try

not to worry about the men. It's likely they've taken shelter somewhere by now."

The cold, damp air rushed in when they opened the door, and Arianna shivered as she watched them from the kitchen window. They quickly disappeared behind the heavy curtains of rain that poured down.

Arianna turned off the lights as she moved toward the front of the resort. Though she'd wanted to be alone and to have time to think, that had been before she'd realized the extent of the danger that Paul might be facing in this terrible storm. Now the beautiful resort was only a hollow shell that echoed her footsteps eerily as she made her way to the lobby. It felt and sounded like her life—empty, lonely, and, on this dark night, more than a little frightening.

Chapter Ten

Crossing the shadowy room, Arianna noted that someone had left a neatly stacked pile of logs in the fireplace and that there was kindling and a container holding long matches. She placed the kindling carefully around the logs and lit the first match. It was several minutes before the logs caught, but once they did, the flames leaped eagerly and the warmth reached out to her, drawing her to settle herself on the love seat. She huddled there, feeling lost and frightened and very much alone in the haunted building. For the first time since Paul's sudden appearance, she had an opportunity to think, and her mind was whirling.

What had Paul meant by saying that she couldn't leave the island without an explanation? He'd been so adamant about the divorce—even admitting that he'd gone to Denver to secure it himself. And what was the "everything" she was to explain?

That question faded in the face of a more frightening thought. Where *was* Paul? Had she seen him tonight only to lose him to an even more permanent kind

of separation? She could hear the waves lashing the
dock even over the heavy wash of the rain. Plagued by
her own fears, she left the love seat and paced to the
window, staring out at the night but seeing nothing
because it was so dark.

Dark! Suddenly the very blackness of the night struck
her. Not sure if it was as bad as she thought, she moved
out onto the deck, shivering in the cold. She could
hardly see the dock even when she moved to the rail.
Immediately she realized the meaning of what she was
seeing. No one could find this cove in the storm, not
without a light as a guide. Cursing herself for a fool for
not having thought of it sooner while Flo and Charles
were still at the resort to help her, she looked around.

There were no lights on the dock, she knew; but
there had to be something she could do. Shaking with
cold and fear, she retreated into the lobby to think.
Then she remembered the storage area off the kitchen
where Flo and Charles had gone to get rain gear for
their walk to the village.

The storage area was a vast confusion, but it didn't
take her long to spot the large self-contained, battery-
operated floodlights. Three of them were stored there,
and a quick check showed her that all three were in
working order. Not sure exactly what she was going to
do, but determined that she had to do something, she
pulled on a hooded slicker and began half-carrying, half-
dragging the first of the floodlights out to the dock.

It was a terrible job, but once she'd secured it to the
end of the dock and turned it on, she felt a small glow
of satisfaction. Somehow it seemed a true beacon, something that would bring Paul back to her through the
frightening darkness.

By the time the second one was in place, her back was aching and she was half-sick from the strain and worry. She struggled along the muddy path back to the resort in a fog of exhaustion, not stopping until she reached the deck. From there she looked back at the dock, trying to decide whether she should use the third light now or keep it in reserve, in case the other two didn't last out the night.

The two floodlights cast an amazing amount of light even in the stormy night. One probed just a little beyond the opening of the cove and the other rose at a higher angle to guide a helicopter in safely. It was enough to bring in the men, if they were on their way home, she decided. Now all she needed to do was keep watch and make sure that the lights continued to offer that hope.

Arianna shed her rain gear on the deck, then returned to the fireplace, curling up on one of the love seats. Her eyes burned and she closed them for a moment, pretending that she was somewhere else, somewhere safe and protected and not so dreadfully alone. The warmth of the fire and the monotonous howl of the wind and the tattoo of the rain blurred her into a kind of waking sleep. She knew where she was, but she was no longer alone. Paul was in the dream world with her, holding her safely in his arms as his fingers slipped softly, gently over her body in a thousand tender caresses.

"I've missed you so much, Arianna," the phantom Paul whispered, his lips moving over her, too. "I've always wanted you here. This will be our world now, our home, our dream come true, and we'll never have to be apart again."

Tears swelled beneath her eyelids and she realized that it was only a dream, a dream that could never

come true. Aching with her weariness and the pain of
her earlier encounter with Paul, Arianna sat up, rub-
bing her eyes and yawning.

The fire was burning lower, she realized, the stack of
logs nearly consumed, which meant she'd been sleeping
for a while. Time to check the lights, she thought,
stifling another yawn. Then she realized something
else. Though the rain still drummed rhythmically on
the roof that extended out over the deck, the wind was
no longer howling or driving the drops like sleet against
the windows.

Arianna tried to see her watch, squinting in the poor
light of the flickering fire, but before she could make
out the numbers, another sound reached her ears.
Her breath caught in her throat as her ears identi-
fied the distant throbbing of a boat motor.

Mr. Woodruff? She scrambled to her feet, wincing
when she realized that one of her legs had gone to
sleep while she had been curled up on the love seat.

The sound grew louder as she limped to the door,
and she was relieved when she opened it and saw that
the floodlights were still burning. Knowing that the old
man would be wet and cold and possibly in need of
help, she ran out, not even bothering to pick up her
discarded rain gear.

The rain was like an icy wave once she left the shelter
of the deck, but she paid no attention to it as she
slipped and slid along the mired path to the dock. "Mr.
Woodruff?" she called. "Mr. Woodruff, is that you?"

The downpour seemed to absorb her words, but as
she neared the dock, she was relieved to see the boat
following the path of the light that she'd aimed at the
cove entrance. Its approach was slow but steady, and as

she reached one end of the dock, the boat bumped lightly against the other end.

The single passenger spent a moment securing the boat to the dock, then climbed wearily out of the boat, leaning for several seconds against the timber post that rose from the corner of the dock before he began limping toward her. Though the hooded slicker obscured his face in the brief moment when he was passing the second floodlight, Adrianna knew at once that it wasn't Mr. Woodruff.

Some instinct deeper and stronger than reason lifted her heart and told her that her wordless prayers had been answered. Relief made her knees weak, and she moved forward slowly, conscious that she must look like a drowned rat after standing in the rain.

"Paul," she cried softly. "Oh, Paul, thank God you're safe!"

"What are you doing out in the rain, Arianna?" he demanded.

"I heard the boat and thought it was Mr. Woodruff. I came to help him inside." Suddenly she realized the implications of Paul returning alone in Mr. Woodruff's boat. "Where—?"

"He's safe in a hospital bed by now," Paul answered.

"Hospital?" Arianna gasped as they slogged up the path to the deck of the resort.

"He was bruised up a bit trying to get the boat ashore on Little Greentop Island, and he was so cold and wet, I asked Dave to take him to the hospital for observation." He chuckled without humor. "I didn't know I was going to have such a rough time getting back here myself or I would have gone with them. If it hadn't been for the lights, I probably would have been wandering till morning. It's a darn good thing they were lit."

They reached the deck and he shed his slicker beside the one she'd abandoned earlier. Arianna opened the door, and the warm dry air of the lobby rushed over her. She walked over and collapsed on the love seat.

"You're half-drowned," he observed accusingly. "What in the hell were you doing running around out there without rain gear?"

"The same thing you were doing—trying to help," she returned angrily. But when she saw the strange, somehow tender look now on his rain-dampened face, her anger faded. With them both safe in the lobby, all she could feel was relief, tremendous relief that after all the horrible hours of waiting, he was finally here and alive. And she knew that the love she so suddenly and overwhelmingly felt must show on her face.

He leaned toward her, his face looking older in the firelight, the marks of strain and weariness clearly etched around his eyes. But his eyes blazed with a fire that matched her own, a fire that had melted her once before, long ago. They still had so much to say to one another—all her anger, all her questions had to be answered—but now, in that warm fire glow, none of the thoughts that had plagued her so incessantly seemed important. The look in his eyes told her that he, too, felt that none of their bitterness or misunderstandings mattered anymore. They were safe, and they were together again after all the long years, and the joy of that was the only thing either of them could feel.

Her eyes were drawn to his lips, and she saw the soft vulnerability of his mouth as it slowly descended toward hers. She moved her gaze back to meet his, and what she read in the glowing depths of his eyes made her lift her slightly parted lips to meet his kiss with an eagerness she couldn't deny.

The kiss was a whirlwind, spinning her back through time, lighting her senses like a candle filling the darkness. Her arms moved around him, feeling the hard contours of the muscles of his back and shoulders under his light knit shirt, moving up to touch the springy, curling hair on his neck, then moving back down to feel the trembling of his back as he clutched her even closer.

"My love, my darling, darling Arianna," he whispered, his lips moving like a firebrand along the quivering ends of her nerves, touching off blazes of delight. Her breath turned to gasping eagerness.

"You're soaked," he murmured, his hands moving between them to unbutton her dripping blouse, pulling it lightly away from her cold, wet skin. His hands brushed the tender skin of her sides as he eased her up. They were warm and rough with the calluses of hard work, yet she felt only a pulsing excitement at his touch. His fingers moved around her, unhooking her wet bra, pulling it, too, away from skin that was no longer cold.

Without thinking, she slipped her hands beneath his shirt, feeling the hot, rippling cords of muscle in his back and shoulders. He moved away from her for a moment, then settled back, his naked chest now warming her further. The thick dark hair on his chest tickled her swelling breasts, bringing further memories of love as his lips found hers in a kiss that robbed her of all thought, filled her with the maddening sensations of desire and passion and a love that she'd denied too long.

His lips moved down her throat to allow his tongue to explore her quivering breasts. Arianna's fingers moved over his still-familiar body, caressing him as he'd taught her, aching with a longing she'd almost forgotten. He groaned as she touched him, then pulled away, staggering to his feet.

"We can't stay here," he whispered, lifting her up and setting her gently on her feet.

For a moment the silence of the room seemed to vibrate; then the last log in the fireplace broke in a flaring of sparks and flames, echoing Arianna's emotions. "Afraid that someone will find us?" she asked, her flesh growing cold even as he held her naked breasts against his own hard-muscled chest.

"My wife doesn't make love on a couch," he replied, a spasm of something very like pain twisting his features. "She belongs in my bed."

The flaring of doubt burned away as she clung to him, her love and passion so intense that she was only slightly aware of being led along the corridor behind the office and into one of the rooms. Paul didn't bother with a light, and she felt the damp coolness of the spread beneath her back as he gently eased her down on his bed.

His hands stripped the rest of her clothing away with ease, yet when his fingers came to caress the soft flesh of her flat stomach, she could feel that they were trembling. She caught his hand and brought it to her lips, first kissing his hard palm, then lightly tracing the lines of his hand with her tongue, tasting the salt of the sea that even the rain hadn't washed away.

His fingers stroked her lips, then moved around to tangle in her wet hair, holding her head still while he once again explored the depths of her mouth so thoroughly that she felt as though he'd tasted her very soul. She moved her own hands down his back, discovering that he, too, was naked, even as his body settled against her quivering, eager flesh.

Memories of pain and joy and emptiness shuddered through her as she rose to meet his questing need, her hands moving on his back as she surrendered to the love she'd never been able to deny. The betrayal was still between them, but this time she felt that she was also betraying herself because she couldn't stop loving the man who held her, who was a very part of her.

"Arianna . . ." Gentle fingers smoothed back the tendrils of her hair.

She returned slowly from the rainbow-hued world of love to the pale room, hearing at first only the pattering of the rain and the soft sounds of breathing beside her. Memory surged over her and she tried to pull away from the tenderly inquisitive fingers. This was a time for talking, not hiding in the passion that had bound them together even after the long separation.

"No." His tone was stern and he held her easily. "I'm not letting you run away again. We have too much to say to each other. I meant to talk to you last night."

"We both meant to talk last night," Arianna agreed, closing her eyes, not wanting to see his face above hers, not wanting to remember the way she'd clung to him, both while they made love and later as she'd slept.

"To begin with, I want to know why—" Paul began, but before he could continue, there was a sharp pounding on the door.

"Paul, you in there?" Charles inquired.

"Be right out," Paul answered.

"I got the radio working, and there's a call for you," Charles informed him. "It's Leila."

"Tell her I'll be there as soon as I get my pants on," Paul called, then swore softly under his breath as he slid out, shivering, to pull on the clothes he'd discarded the night before.

"I'll be right back," he whispered, his eyes meeting Arianna's as she watched him.

Leila! Arianna felt a twisting in her stomach that left her stunned after the door closed behind Paul. She lay still for a moment, then pushed back the quilt, feeling the icy air on her skin. She almost enjoyed it. She felt that the cold was cleaning away the heat of the night.

It took her only a moment to pull on her slacks, but when she looked around for her blouse, she remembered that it must still be lying in the lobby where Paul had dropped it. Cringing, she realized that it was not dawn, as she'd first thought, but nearly midmorning. The Coventrys would be up and the staff would be moving about the resort, finding her clothing.

For a minute, she stood where she was, feeling defeated. She couldn't venture out into the corridor without a top, and she certainly didn't want to wait for Paul's return. She had no doubt that Leila would tell him about her charade, might even be doing it now. She could picture them having a big laugh over it.

She closed her eyes so that she wouldn't have to look at the tumbled bed she'd just left. He must feel as sick as she did, she thought wearily. Or was she wrong to believe he was sensitive? Last night's moments of tenderness seemed a lifetime ago, and she was no longer sure of anything.

Shivering, she opened the closet door, half-hoping to find something feminine hanging inside, but the collection of clothing was strictly masculine. She touched the clothes lightly, a moment of longing washing over her; then she pulled a bright green knit shirt off its hanger and put it on.

Still unready to venture into the hall and take the chance of meeting someone, she stepped into the small bath to check her reflection in the mirror. The result was depressing. The shirt looked like what it was— borrowed and much too big for her slender frame. Her hair was an impossible tangle, the result of having been soaking wet, then dried while she slept.

Only her face betrayed the other side of her nature. Her skin glowed and she saw the longing that still swept through her at the memories of Paul's kisses. Right or wrong, love or hate, she had the horrible suspicion that Paul could come in at this moment and claim her love once more.

Using her fingers, she combed her hair as much as she could, then left the mirror and went to the door, opening it only an inch to peek out at the corridor. It appeared deserted, so she hurried to her own door. She opened it, slipped inside, then locked it with shaking fingers. No one was pounding on its panels, demanding entrance, but she felt as though she'd escaped a deadly pursuit.

Her room was dark, since she'd closed the curtains early in the afternoon and hadn't returned to open them. She didn't bother to turn on the light, however and crossed directly to the bathroom. She turned on the hot shower even before she stripped off her slacks and Paul's shirt. The hot water washed the tangles from her hair, but it couldn't smooth away the feel of Paul's hands on her flesh, the invisible marks that his body had left on hers. She soaped herself twice and stood beneath the coursing water till she thought her skin must be wrinkled as a prune. Finally, however, she turned off the water and wrapped herself in the thick, fluffy towels.

What was she going to do? she asked herself as she apologetically lathered her body with lotion to make up for so much washing. It was too late to simply retreat and leave everything to a lawyer, wasn't it? She looked down at her rosy, glowing body and shivered, though the bathroom was steamy. Last night had certainly proved that she wasn't capable of denying her feelings for Paul.

Sighing, she put on her robe, then turned her attention to her hair, trying to concentrate on fixing it, and not on her memories. She still wanted to face Leila, she decided. She felt that she deserved some sort of explanation for the redhead's actions, if only for her own peace of mind. Arianna returned to her bedroom and switched on the small dressing-table lamp. She looked around, wincing at the sight of her neatly made bed; then she gasped.

Her blouse and bra lay on the brightly patterned bedspread like an accusation. Arianna looked at them guiltily. Who could have put them here? she asked herself. One of the maids? Flo? Mrs. Coventry? None of the answers appealed to her in the slightest. What must they have thought? She knew the answer, and it made her blush; then suddenly she had to giggle. Why was she feeling so guilty and embarrassed? she asked herself. After all, separated or not, she was still Paul Roarke's wife.

The tap on her door made her jump with alarm, and it was a moment before her voice was stable enough to ask, "Who is it?"

"It's me, Arianna," Flo answered.

Arianna opened the door. "I was just getting dressed."

"I was wondering if you'd like something to eat," Flo said. "Maybe some breakfast?"

"Breakfast?" Arianna gulped. She was starving, but she was also loath to face the curious eyes that she suspected would be waiting for her.

"Would you like me to bring you something?" Flo asked. "We're setting up the dining room for lunch, but we won't serve till after the *Star* gets in, so it could be quite a while."

"Would you mind?" Arianna let her breath out in a sigh. "I'm starving, but I look like a drowned rat after being out in the storm last night."

"Hey, it's the least I can do after Charles and I went off and left you alone here last night. If you hadn't thought about using those lights on the dock ... We should have thought of them ourselves, but we were so sure that David and Paul had already taken shelter, we never even considered it."

"Have you heard anything about them?" Arianna asked. "Mr. Woodruff and David, I mean. They did get back safely, didn't they?"

Flo's laughter was warm and easy. "Mr. Woodruff called this morning to make sure that we'd extend his reservation. He's going to miss several days of fishing while he's in the hospital and he wants to make sure he has time enough to make up for it when he gets back."

Arianna laughed too, her own problems forgotten for the moment. "I'm glad," she said, crossing to take clean clothes out of her suitcase. "I was awfully worried about him last night."

"What would you like to eat?" Flo asked, changing the subject.

"Whatever you have left from breakfast," Arianna answered. "People who sleep halfway to noon don't deserve any better.

"You deserve the best," Flo told her as she left.

The happy glow of the news about Mr. Woodruff faded as quickly as it had come, and even remembering what Flo had said about the lights being so important to Paul's safety didn't help. She put on a pair of green-and-brown heather-tweed slacks and a soft dark green sweater that brought out the paleness of her hair and accented her dark eyes. Once she was dressed, she looked around her room and considered disturbing the bed, but it seemed too devious. The time for games was past, she told herself sternly. If anyone asked, she would tell the truth.

Flo's knock interrupted her musing, and she opened the door. The tray was heavy and the scents that rose from it divine. She thanked the waitress with heartfelt gratitude, then carried the food to the small table that sat before the window. The world beyond the window had grown considerably lighter since she'd awakened, and as she ate the eggs, sausage, and English muffins, the wind herded the last of the rain clouds out of her view and the sun began trying to dry up last night's puddles. By the time she'd finished the carafe of coffee, the day was golden and she had a feeling that her sweater would be too warm.

Arianna changed to a long-sleeved shirt, then took a deep breath and picked up her tray. It was time to face the outside world, she told herself. She couldn't hide forever in her room.

Chapter Eleven

The kitchen was a beehive of activity, but a quick glance told her that the tall dark-haired man she was seeking wasn't among the hurrying figures that moved there, so she simply thanked Charles for the breakfast and went through the dining room to the lobby. The contrast was a shock. The big room was empty and quiet.

Feeling both curious and embarrassed, Arianna crossed to the love seats, half-expecting to find some sign of last night's magical moments there. But even the ashes of her fire were gone, and a new pile of logs awaited the cool of evening.

"Good morning." Mrs. Coventry was coming down the stairs. "I see you survived the storm all right," she continued, her open smile making Arianna sure that she, at least, had not been the one to find the blouse and bra.

"Barely," she replied. "How are you and your husband this morning? I suppose he's feeling very pleased at having forecast correctly about the storm."

"He's not happy about the storm," Mrs. Coventry

153

replied. "In fact, he's out with Mr. Roarke inspecting damage." She shook her head. "We were so relieved to hear that Mr. Woodruff is safe. It must have been very close, them snatching him off that tiny speck of an island just before the waves swamped it."

Arianna couldn't hide her amazement. "Is that what happened?" she asked, feeling foolish. "I didn't hear the details last night, just that he was safe."

"Oh, my, yes, it is quite a story. Of course, Mr. Roarke wasn't willing to tell it, but my husband managed to pry it out of him. Seems they were running low on fuel in the helicopter when they spotted the boat on a tiny island. In fact, they weren't sure they had enough fuel to get back to the hospital with three men on board, so Mr. Roarke said he'd bring the boat to Pellington and let the pilot take Mr. Woodruff on to the hospital alone."

"It must have been terrible," Arianna acknowledged, remembering the wildness of the night and her own desperate fears. It was frightening to realize how close to the truth her worst imaginings had been.

"According to Mr. Roarke, he might not have made it if he hadn't seen the lights on the dock, the lights you put there." Mrs. Coventry's gaze narrowed slightly. "How did you know that you should do that?" she asked. "Mr. Roarke didn't know, and I would never have thought of such a thing myself."

Arianna shrugged. "My father always flew his own plane, and he used to tell me stories about the natives setting out lights or building small fires around the back-country landing strips for him. I didn't know that Paul was in a boat. I was really setting the lights out to guide the helicopter to the dock."

"Well, whatever the reason, you did the right thing, that's for sure." Mrs. Coventry smiled at her. "Mr. Roarke said so often enough while we were talking. I guess he'd just found out who set out the lights."

Arianna felt a blush rising in her cheeks. "Do you know when they'll be back?" she asked. "Paul and your husband, I mean."

Mrs. Coventry shook her head. "I have no idea. One of the young men came into the dining room looking upset when we were talking to Mr. Roarke. Mr. Roarke went to speak with him for a few minutes. They both seemed so disturbed while they were talking, that my husband went to ask if he could help. They left a few minutes later, saying something about inspecting for storm damage."

Arianna nodded, doing her best to hide her disappointment and relief. Her feelings were still so chaotic, it seemed her every response was a combination of two opposing emotions. She longed to see him again and at the same time was almost afraid to face him.

Mrs. Coventry moved past Arianna and went to the window. "Look, isn't that the boat?" she called to Arianna. Arianna joined Mrs. Coventry and stared out at the bright world, watching as the familiar shape of the *Pellington Star* came into view around the tip of land that protected the cove. Other, older memories quickened her heartbeat; then it slowed as she realized that the boat's arrival meant only that Leila would be back on the island—and before she'd had a chance to talk to Paul.

"Shall we go down to the dock and welcome everyone back?" Mrs. Coventry suggested.

"You go ahead," Arianna told her. "I'd better stick

with the desk. I've neglected my duties enough for one day." She tried to make the statement sound light and teasing, but she could tell from the older woman's eyes that she hadn't been quite convincing.

Mrs. Coventry left and Arianna tried to force herself to do as she'd said and return to the desk and office, but something about the scene outside held her prisoner. The *Star* moved with grace toward the dock, looking almost unchanged since the first time she'd seen it that long-ago day in Seattle. She could see the crowd of guests at the rail and even Leila's glowing red hair as she waved wildly to . . .

Paul moved into Arianna's field of vision as he stepped out on the dock. Arianna swallowed hard. He'd evidently returned to his room, for he was now wearing dark brown slacks and a bright yellow shirt, not the stained Levi's he'd pulled on to answer the radio call.

Paul caught the rope that was thrown to him by a crew member and helped to secure the boat. Then he stood on the dock welcoming the passengers as they came ashore. Arianna watched, envying the guests their moments of casual conversation with him. She was aware that she should do something, but she was unwilling to leave the window even long enough to alert the kitchen staff that the guests were back.

It wasn't till the crowd on the dock thinned that Arianna realized that Leila hadn't come ashore. Frowning, she searched the deck area of the *Star*. Paul, too, seemed to be looking for her, for he went aboard the boat.

Leila came out of the cabin immediately, and in a moment she was in Paul's arms, his dark head bent down to meet her bright one. Arianna left the window abruptly, moving quickly until the phone rang. For two rings she tried to ignore it, reasoning that answering it wasn't her job, never had been in actual fact, but habit was too strong, and on the third ring she picked up the receiver. "Pellington Island Resort," she said, her voice quivering only slightly.

"Just retesting the phone lines, ma'am," a voice told her. "We had to shut the system down for a while and we wanted to be sure that you were back in operation."

"Oh, thank you." Arianna waited to hear the click, then replaced the receiver. She started to go to her room, but before she could make her escape, the friendly guests were all around her. They were soon telling her their stories about the storm and asking her for details about what had happened on the island while they were safe in Victoria.

Leila entered the building before Arianna had managed to leave, and their eyes met across the crowded lobby. Arianna swallowed hard, for there was no friendliness in Leila's eyes now, only cold anger. Still, they had no chance to talk privately, for the guests required their attention. It wasn't until everyone but Arianna went in to lunch that she realized that Paul hadn't returned to the resort building. Since she had no appetite for food, Arianna went outside where one of the young men was washing the mud off the resort deck.

"Have you seen Paul?" she asked.

"Oh, he went with Mike Jeffers," the young man answered.

"Went where?" Arianna asked, suddenly realizing that the *Pellington Star* was no longer tied up at the dock.

"Emergency call, I guess." He shrugged. "They just refueled and left."

Paul's earnest words about their having to talk filled

her mind, and she almost shook with frustration. The storm that had brought them together so violently last night now seemed to be determined to separate them just as quickly, leaving nothing solved.

"Are you all right?" the young man asked.

"I'm just tired," Arianna answered, pulling herself together and retreating to the now quiet lobby. Perhaps it was an omen, she thought wearily. Maybe it was time to leave this place. She went behind the desk and started through the office.

"Just a moment."

Arianna stopped, chilled by the cold voice as she turned to see that Leila had emerged from the dining room and was now standing on the far side of the desk. "What do you want?" she asked.

"In the office," Leila snapped, coming around the desk and closing the door. "Close the hall door, I want to talk to you."

Arianna hesitated, aware that she and Leila had a confrontation coming, but wanting more time to think before she had to face her. To her surprise, the redhead moved past her and slammed the door herself.

"What do you think you're doing here, Miss Kane?" she demanded. "Why did you come, anyway? Didn't you hurt Paul enough the first time?"

"I don't know what you're talking about," Arianna gasped, totally confused by the attack.

"Don't give me that," Leila grated. "I recognized you as soon as you gave your name, or anyway soon after. I just couldn't figure out what you were after. Now I think I'm beginning to understand."

"Understand what?" Arianna was too caught by her own curiosity about the redhead to return her attack.

"You aren't a rich heiress after all, so you came here to see what Paul had to offer, didn't you? Well, you can just forget about taking this place away from him. You deserted Paul five years ago and we built this together, so you can't claim any part of it." As she continued to speak, Leila moved about the small room touching desk, files, even the walls with possessive fingers. "It's my life, too," she went on. "I care about him and he cares for me. We did this together."

Arianna stared at her, bewildered. "You think I came here to take this away from Paul?"

Leila's burning gaze fell before Arianna's shocked stare. "That's what I decided you were after when you came pretending to be a girl from the agency just looking for a job," she said in a slightly less belligerent tone.

"I came here to see Paul," Arianna began, controlling her own anger firmly. "When he wasn't here on the island, I decided to wait for him. You were the one who assumed that I was a secretary."

"You didn't deny it."

Arianna said nothing for a moment, studying the woman before her. "If you knew who I was," she asked, "why didn't you say something at the time?"

"I wanted to know why you were here," Leila answered at last, her expression changing. "I saw what you did to Paul the first time. I thought I owed it to him to find out what you were up to this time. I couldn't let you destroy everything."

Arianna looked deep into Leila's hazel eyes and saw an echo of her own pain there; then she remembered the embrace she'd witnessed from the window. She took a deep, shuddering breath. "You love him, don't you?" she asked very softly.

Leila opened her mouth, then closed it without speaking. She nodded.

"And he cares for you?" Arianna tried not to remember last night's wild abandon, the joy and the magic that had nearly shattered them both as they renewed their loving.

"We've been happy here together," Leila answered.

"Well, you will be again," Arianna said quietly, hoping that her voice wouldn't break and display the agony the words cost her. "I was just on my way to pack my suitcase. When Paul decides to come back, you can tell him that his resort is safe. My attorney will ask only that the marriage be dissolved. I want nothing from Paul."

Leila's eyes flashed once with triumph; then the glow was gone and she suddenly looked older and as weary as Arianna felt. "There's no point in your packing today, Arianna," Leila informed her. "There's no way off the island unless you want to call for a seaplane, and you might not even get one of them before tomorrow. The storm did a lot of damage and stranded a lot of people. There are boats missing and people needing help all over the area. The ferry won't come before tomorrow at the earliest. It may not even start regular service till next week."

"And what about Paul?" It was a question she couldn't stop herself from asking. "When will he be back?"

Leila shrugged. "There's no way of knowing."

"Could he be here tonight?" Arianna asked.

"I honestly don't know."

"If he will be back, I'd rather not stay here."

"There's nowhere else for you to go," Leila said. "All the cabins are filled. There's nothing available in the village." She sighed. "A couple of houses were damaged by the storm, so people there are doubling up just for shelter."

Arianna thought sadly of an abandoned barn, wondering bitterly if it was still standing. But she had been a child then, a frightened girl fleeing from feelings she didn't understand. She was no longer that confused girl. She would behave as an adult, staying here until she could leave with dignity. She had, after all, come to find the answers to her questions; she had no right to complain because she didn't like what she had learned.

Arianna drew herself up to her full five-six, straightening her shoulders and tossing back her golden mane. "I'll stay until some sort of transport can be arranged," she told Leila. "If you could let me know as soon as you hear of anything . . ."

"I'll do my best to arrange something," Leila replied, her eyes watching Arianna in a new way—wary, yet respectful.

"Thank you." Arianna left the office without hurrying, though she longed to flee down the corridor and throw herself on her bed to cry. This time, however, her eyes only burned with dry pain, beyond tears.

Arianna packed carefully, leaving out what she would need for the rest of the day and the night. Weary after the strain of the storm's terror and her own personal upheaval, she lay down on her bed and tried to sleep, but her memories kept intruding. Though she finally managed to banish Paul from her thoughts, she couldn't completely ignore the replay of the scene she'd had with Leila.

How had she caused Paul pain, hurt him the way
Leila claimed? She searched her mind for clues, but she
could find none. Perhaps Leila had been a victim of
some lie that Paul had told her about his ill-starred
marriage. The thought took root painfully, for to ac-
cuse him of such duplicity was to admit that she'd given
her heart to a man beneath contempt. Yet in a way, it
did make sense. He certainly wouldn't have admitted to
seducing an innocent girl into marriage so that he
could get money from her father.

But what about Leila? Arianna asked herself. How
much had she contributed to the resort? Had he used
her obvious feelings for him to . . . ? But that was too
monstrous to be believed. Besides, she told herself wryly,
Leila was much more able to take care of herself than
Arianna had been five years ago.

That sobering thought made her banish all speculation.
It was time to drop the past and begin to think about
the future, she told herself. The small trust-fund in-
come she was to receive would be enough for a while,
but it was nothing to build a life on. Besides, the empty
years that stretched ahead of her needed dreams and
plans to fill them. Otherwise, she knew she'd never be
able to leave the ashes of her past behind.

Sleep overcame her before she'd formulated anything beyond a hazy idea of returning to school to take
a course in business management or perhaps even resort management. Pretending to work here for a day
had been exciting and challenging, and there were
things that she'd noticed that could be improved, ideas
that she'd thought she might discuss with Paul.

It was midafternoon when she awoke. Sunlight still
beamed down outside, making the dimness of her room

seem oppressive, yet she felt no desire to venture out to the lobby or dining room. She didn't want another confrontation with Leila. She brushed her hair into a semblance of order and changed to sturdy tennis shoes, deciding that a walk to the village was in order. Though she told herself that she was making the long hike to check on the ferry schedules, deep inside she knew that her reasons were far more complex. All of Pellington Island had a part in her memories, and since she would never have the opportunity to visit it again, she felt a strong urge to see the village one last time. Besides, she told herself as she slipped her wallet into her jacket pocket, if she had an early dinner at the Grotto, she could successfully avoid eating in the resort dining room, where she would be sure to meet Leila. She slipped out the rear door and crossed the deck to step down on the still-damp grass.

The air was sweet with the scents of a new-washed world, but Arianna wasn't aware of it. Nor did she feel the mud that slithered under her feet as she made her way between the cabins, seeking the path to the village. It was the same path she'd followed that night that seemed a lifetime ago, but it was also as changed by the years as she was.

Tall pines still shadowed it, but there were ruts now from the vehicles that came and went from village to resort and back again. Grass no longer grew so thickly, and there were fewer wildflowers close to the path. Too many feet passing back and forth as people from the village came to work each morning and returned home each night. She smiled sadly, remembering Paul's dream of keeping the young people on the island by supplying jobs. It seemed to have worked out just the way he'd hoped.

The village surprised her, not by the changes, but by the way it had stayed the same. Arianna paused at the edge of the forest. The once-deserted barn was empty and abandoned no longer. Someone had converted it to a home, and she had a feeling that water no longer dripped from the roof during a cold and rainy night.

Sighing, she went down the slight incline to the village, wandering the streets, seeing the damage that Leila had mentioned. A dead pine had been toppled by the storm, taking a part of a nearby building with it. A shed roof had been torn off. Signs were stripped from the stores, and several windows had been boarded up to cover the broken glass. People milled about, busily cleaning away the debris of the storm, seeming none the worse for the terrible night. Arianna wandered among them with a smile, pleased that her expression was answered in kind; she felt almost as though she could belong here, and it brought her bittersweet pain.

The Grotto was nearly empty, and Arianna felt a little conspicuous being shown to a table all alone. "You must be from the resort," the middle-aged proprietor observed as she brought Arianna a glass of white wine.

Arianna nodded.

"Bet you've seen my daughter out there," the woman continued, leaning on a nearby table. "My Flo is their top waitress. I trained her right here. In a couple of years, she's going to be in charge of that resort dining room, I bet."

"I expect you're right," Arianna agreed, realizing now that the woman did look something like the helpful and friendly waitress. "She's very nice and efficient, too."

"You know her, then?" The woman sank down in a chair, obviously ready to talk, which pleased Arianna, since she'd felt rather lonely.

"I was helping out for a day or so," she explained, "working at the desk while they were shorthanded. That's how I got to know Flo fairly well—especially during the storm."

"Preston picked a bad time to break his leg," the woman agreed. "What do you think of the resort they've built out there?"

"It's most impressive," Arianna answered, suddenly curious about what this woman might know about Leila, Paul, and the resort.

"Pretty grand for Pellington, I'd say. Nothing like my little Grotto. Guess old Meg's place just isn't good enough anymore."

"Oh, come now, don't you get business from the people who stay at the resort?" Arianna asked.

"Sure, but it's not the same. I told Paul's father that it was a mistake to let Paul build it, but he wouldn't listen. Said Paul had worked hard for his dream, he couldn't deny him the right to see it come to life."

"He worked hard for it?" Arianna couldn't keep the doubt from showing in her voice. She forced a smile, hoping that the woman wouldn't guess her thoughts.

"Sounds to me like you knew him before he got ambition," Meg observed. "Playboy Paul, we used to call him. Floating around the area in his fancy boat with all his tourists. Never did get straight what made him start building that resort, but it must have been something pretty powerful."

The woman stopped and looked expectantly at Arianna, but she had no words for her. After a moment Meg went on. "Never saw a man more driven. Working night and day, he was, dragging his daddy into it, his mom. They were happy with their fish camp, but not Paul. No, he had to have something much grander. I still think that's why his folks moved away—they were tired of working all the time."

"My goodness, I had no idea that Paul . . ." Arianna began, then let it trail off as the door of the restaurant opened and an older couple came in.

Meg struggled to her feet and went to greet the new customers, leaving Arianna to ponder her revelations. Maybe her father's payoff to Paul had been so small that it had only started the resort, and there had been a promise of more to come after the divorce—an offer that Paul had, for some reason, chosen to reject. It was a strange idea, yet it fit the things she'd heard better than any other explanation had. The problem was, it didn't make things any easier to understand. If Paul had been willing to sell out their marriage for money, why hadn't he been willing to go all the way?

Meg returned, but only long enough to take Arianna's dinner order and to refill her wineglass. A couple of young women came in and settled at a nearby table, giggling and talking about someone called Gary. Arianna listened idly, remembering the years when she and Joy had been together in just that way, talking and giggling.

Oddly enough, thinking of Joy brought Leila to her mind, and she felt a pang of regret. Under other circumstances, they might have become friends. She shook her head, realizing that such thoughts were foolish.

After tomorrow she would never see any of them again. She would never again explore this lovely, special island.

Tears stung her eyes and she was glad when Meg arrived with her salad. The wine, she told herself—that was all that was making her so sentimental. The new Arianna wasn't going to be sentimental. The new Arianna was going to be brave and strong and tough. Love would never trap her into making a fool of herself.

"You staying on the island long, miss?" Meg asked as she brought the salmon dinner Arianna had ordered.

"That depends on whether or not the ferry will be running tomorrow," Arianna answered. "That's why I came into the village. Would you happen to know about that?"

"You'll have to check on the dock, but my guess is that there won't be a ferry for a couple more days. Last I heard, they sustained some damage during the storm and were being towed into Nanaimo for repairs."

Arianna groaned, thinking of the added expense of summoning the seaplane. Unless they were making a scheduled stop, it could be expensive. She smiled to herself wryly, realizing that this was the first time in her life that she'd ever had to consider the cost of anything.

"Might be you'll get someone to pick you up when they bring guests to the resort," Meg suggested. "Leila's good at arranging things like that."

"I'm sure she'll try real hard," Arianna observed with bitter humor. "Thanks for the suggestion."

She ate slowly, savoring the food and the ease of being in this place where no one knew her. Once she'd finished a final glass of wine and paid her bill, she wandered back out to the street, noting that the sun was now low on the horizon. Time to be starting back, though she planned to walk very slowly, hoping to arrive when everyone else was at dinner.

Her brief visit to the dock area confirmed Meg's warning about the ferry, and she started back to the resort feeling very much as though she was trapped on the island. The feeling wasn't helped when she reached the resort clearing and saw that the dock area was no longer empty. The *Pellington Star* had returned.

Chapter Twelve

Arianna hesitated on the edge of the forest, her heart-beat quickening at the sight of the boat, then slowing again as she reminded herself that she had made her decision. Leila had been right to tell her she had no place in Paul's life now and the best way to avoid seeing him would be to stay away from the resort as much as possible.

She moved carefully along the tree line, pausing in the deep shadows to stare at the scene beyond the lighted windows of the dining room. The spacious room was nearly filled. She could see Flo and the other waitresses moving quickly between the tables, serving the guests. Arianna moved closer, trying to peer between the diners to find out if Paul and Leila were eating with their guests tonight.

The redhead was fairly easy to locate, and after a moment Arianna saw Paul's profile as he leaned close to speak to her. She forced herself to turn away, moving back to the stairway that gave access to the deck, then following it around to the side entrance, heading along the corridor to her room.

Her room looked much as she'd left it except for a scrap of white paper on the dresser. The note on it was short and to the point.

> Arianna,
> > We have to talk.
> > > > > > Paul

She held it for a moment, a part of her aglow with excitement at this evidence of his feeling, while another part felt only fear. What if he should come back again, should take her in his arms? Her racing pulse gave her the answer that she dreaded. But where could she hide? It was far too late to go back to the village, and there was no place in the resort where she could be confident of avoiding him. Frustration warred with anticipation, an unsettling combination. She couldn't stay here, she realized fearfully.

Knowing that the night would quickly cool now that the sun had vanished, she changed into wool slacks and a sweater, then picked up her jacket. She retraced her steps, leaving the building by the side door. The evening was cool, but bright, with a nearly full moon rising beyond the cove. She followed a pale path that led across the lawn, past the cabins, and into the forest. The night breeze combed through her hair with delicate fingers, cooling the fever that thoughts of Paul had brought to her cheeks.

The path became dimmer as the forest closed in around her, but Arianna felt no fear, only a kind of weary lassitude. During those magical honeymoon days of love they had talked so often of living here, of loving here, that she still felt welcomed by the land. This island was a part of the Paul that she'd known and loved; the Paul that had loved her, however briefly.

The glow of moonlight came from ahead of her, and Arianna walked faster, drawn to it. Her breath caught in her throat as she stepped out into the clearing. Lush grass swayed sensuously as the breeze caressed it, and everywhere she could see the pale gleam of wildflowers. Their light, delicate fragrance tickled her nostrils.

Entranced, Arianna looked around till she spotted the dark bulk of a huge fallen tree. Crossing to it, she touched the old wood and was pleased to find that the day's sun had dried it enough for her to sit down. She settled herself with a sigh of contentment.

After a few moments a soft rustling startled her, and she peered across the moonlit expanse of grass to the shadowy cavern of the forest. For a heartbeat she could see nothing; then a dark shape emerged and moved cautiously into the open. Arianna caught her breath, unable to believe her eyes as the graceful doe began to graze on the deep grass while her fawn wandered about exploring the clearing.

Arianna sat very still, almost holding her breath, afraid of frightening the beautiful creatures. Time seemed to stand still as the doe grazed and the fawn frolicked in the moonlight. Suddenly Arianna stiffened, her sharp ears catching the sound of movement behind her. She started to rise, but a warm hand touched her arm and Paul settled himself beside her on the fallen log.

Though she'd expected the deer to flee at his approach, when she turned her attention back to the meadow,

Arianna saw that the doe was actually coming toward them. To her surprise, Paul extended his hand and she saw that there was a piece of apple resting in his palm.

The doe approached cautiously, but she took the apple from his hand. Without a word, Paul gave Arianna several bits of fruit, smiling as she shyly offered them to the velvet-nosed deer.

"I can't believe this is really happening," Arianna breathed when the apple was all gone and the doe had returned to her grazing, her fawn watching them curiously from the safety of his mother's side. "They're so tame."

Paul's low chuckle was like a caress. "We have six or seven deer on the island," he explained. "Every fall someone brings us a wounded victim of the hunters. Those we can save live out their lives here. And we occasionally get an orphaned fawn in the spring. We offer them a safe sanctuary, and after a while, they learn to trust us."

"How wonderful," Arianna breathed, her eyes leaving the graceful doe and turning to look at Paul. "They're so gentle and beautiful, I don't see why anyone would want to kill them."

Paul's expression grew sad. "My father took me hunting when I was just sixteen. It seemed like the most exciting thing that had ever happened to me. I was proud of the rifle he'd given me, and very anxious to prove myself a man in my father's eyes." Paul paused, wiping his hands on his handkerchief. Arianna nodded encouragingly, quite able to picture the boy that Paul must have been. "Everything was terrific. I loved camping out in the woods with a couple of my father's friends, learning to track, stalking the deer. Then the moment arrived." He stopped again, seeming lost in thought. Arianna waited, unwilling to speak and break the mood of trust and communication that was spreading between them. "I came upon a beautiful buck grazing in a meadow a lot like this one. I was just ready to shoot when something spooked him. He leaped away just as I fired. It was a remarkable shot according to my father and his friends."

This time his silence had a different quality, and Arianna felt the need to break it by asking, "Did you kill the buck?"

Paul nodded. "That was what was so terrific about my shot. It was a clean kill, instant death for the deer." His eyes met hers in the clarity of the moonlight.

Paul reached out to her, his fingers touching her cheek lightly. "Dear Arianna, you look just the way I felt when I stood looking down at that buck, seeing him dead, when only a moment before he'd been alive and full of vitality." His face was sad. "My father never forgave me for just walking away from the hunting party. He couldn't understand why I never used my rifle again."

"And now you offer them sanctuary here," Arianna whispered, deeply moved by the story and all that it revealed about this stranger she loved so intensely.

"I don't like hurting things," he continued. "I never have, Arianna, not animals . . . and more especially, not people."

Arianna stiffened, his words destroying the enchantment of the moment, reminding her as they did of all the hurt she'd suffered from his betrayal five years ago. "I'd better be getting back," she began, but his hand dropped from her face to her shoulder, holding her lightly but firmly.

"I don't pretend to know what's going on with you, Arianna, but I do know one thing. We have to talk. We have some things to settle between us, and I'm not letting you leave this island until we do it."

"You can't hold me prisoner here," Arianna protested, reacting violently to the surge of joy that threatened to melt her stern resolve to cut this man out of her life for good.

"That's where you're wrong," Paul informed her, his tone slightly mocking. "The only boat that will be coming and going from Pellington Island for the next few days is the *Star*, and Mike takes her out only on *my* orders."

"And you say that you don't like to hurt people." The words came out on a tide of bitterness.

She saw his reaction in his face. He seemed to feel the words like a blow, and for a heartbeat she was afraid that he was going to retaliate. His hand moved from her shoulder to the back of her head, tangling in her hair. Before she could stop him, his lips descended to claim hers.

The kiss, tender at first, quickly intensified as the magic of the night and the setting breached the defenses she'd erected. Her lips opened beneath his and her arms lifted to hold him, her fingers curling in his hair and caressing the swell of his lean back muscles as he pulled her even closer. The kiss was endless, leaving her breathless and aching with all the desire he'd fulfilled the night before. His hands moved restlessly along her back; then one curved around her to caress her swollen breast through the soft knit of her sweater.

"Why do you keep denying your feelings, Arianna?" he asked. "You showed me last night that you still love me, so why do you keep running away?"

All the reasons, the questions, the answers she'd wanted swirled through her mind, but they were unimportant in the face of the emotions that were tearing at her. Last night's blazing passion had been a mere prelude to what washed over her now. Suddenly nothing was more important than this moment, the man holding her in his arms, and the magic of all that still pulsed like electricity between them.

Paul stood up, pulling her with him so that her body was pressed against the hard length of him. She moved closer, hating the thickness of the cloth that still kept them apart as her own hands slid down to press his loins more tightly against her.

"I'm not running away," she told him, her eyes meeting his in the glow of moonlight.

"There was never anyone like you, Arianna," he whispered as they moved away from the log, crossing the meadow, oblivious of the flight of the startled doe and fawn. He seemed to move from light to darkness without hesitation. Arianna didn't care where they were going; she'd made her choice, she was with him. She let her lips move slowly along the side of his neck, tasting the tang of his after-shave and the slight saltiness of his perspiration.

He paused at last, his lips reclaiming hers, his hands clasping her tight to him once again. His kiss was like a swelling tide in her body, leaving her knees weak, her head spinning, and her body pulsing with a passionate need for more, always more.

Arianna was dimly aware that they were on some sort

of porch; then a door opened and they were inside. The cabin! She gazed at the dark room as he led her to the bed.

His hands moved over her, gently removing her clothing. His lips followed his fingers, and the coolness of the air on her naked flesh was burned away by the raging heat of her response as she fumbled with the buttons on his shirt. After she had stripped his clothes away, he eased her down on the soft bed. Arianna tried to will herself to deny him now, at the moment when his desire for her was the most potent. She wanted to make him hurt and ache for her as she'd ached for him the past five years. But his fingers were liquid flames licking her very nerves, sending ripples of pleasure to her breasts, her thighs, to the secret recesses of her body.

Moaning with the pain of her betrayed love for him, she lifted her body to receive his thrusting desire, not in surrender, but in demanding passion. She might never see him again, but for this moment he was hers, and she meant to drown in that fiery caldron of love.

The coolness of the night air on her damp, naked flesh brought her back to reality as Paul sat up. She opened her eyes, but there was nothing to be seen, for the darkness of the cabin was complete. Somehow that seemed appropriate, she thought bitterly. The kind of love that they'd just made belonged in darkness.

"Now will you admit that you love me?" Paul asked, his voice low and hoarse, his hands moving to caress her lightly, sliding along her sides to settle on the narrow flesh of her waist, making her shiver in spite of her self-hatred.

"Was that what you wanted to prove?" Arianna

demanded, her own voice strange to her ears. "Is that why you insist on keeping me here? Just to show me that you can still make me feel this way? What does that prove to you?"

"Prove?" His tone was suddenly cool. "I didn't know that we were trying to prove anything. I just wanted to tell you—"

"No!" She forced herself to draw away from him. "This time you're going to listen to me, Paul. I've got some things to say to you before you start with your lies and excuses."

Paul stirred but said nothing.

Arianna took a deep breath, dozens of accusations and complaints filling her mind. Firmly, coldly, she forced them all away. "I don't want to wallow in the past, Paul," she began quietly. "I came here only to discuss the divorce that my father led me to believe was granted five years ago."

She stopped, wishing suddenly for light so that she could read what was in his face. He made no sound, didn't even move as he waited for her to go on.

"I won't pretend that I understand why you were willing to sell our love in the first place," she continued, "but not to grant me the freedom you promised was truly unfair. But that's over. I realize now that I can't live in the past. I want to go ahead, and that means leaving the past, you, and this island behind. I'll leave in the morning and have my attorney contact your attorney once I get back to Denver."

Arianna stopped, aware that she was shaking from the effort of keeping her voice calm and steady. Now the words were out, she was grateful for the darkness that hid her agony from Paul.

"What the hell are you talking about?" Paul's tone was startling in its fury. "You run off the moment Daddy beckons, and you say I sold out? What about the way you became Arianna Kane again?"

He paused, but she couldn't answer the accusation he seemed to be leveling at her.

"What was the problem, Arianna? Wouldn't my name bring the headwaiters running or open all those fancy doors for you? You dropped it fast enough."

The vicious attack was like a splash of cold water, echoing as it did some of the things that Leila had said. "Where were you?" she demanded in self-defense. "Why didn't you come back to the boat that day? I waited and waited. Daddy told me that you'd never come, but I didn't believe him. I trusted our love, but you never came back."

"How long did you wait? Two hours, three?" His tone was bitter.

"All day and all night," Arianna snapped. Then after a moment she asked, "Where were you, Paul? What happened? What did Daddy tell you or give you that made you change?"

"Your old man gave me hell, that's what he gave me. He was quite a talker. He told me that I was a gold digger, that I'd married you for his money, but that I wasn't going to get a dime. He informed me that if I ever tried to see you again, he'd have me tossed in jail. Then he left me in a little bar to think it all over."

"You really believed that he'd do that?" Arianna asked, confused by the difference in what Paul was saying and the things her father had told her that day long ago. "Did you think that I'd let him, Paul? He was just angry."

"He saw to it that I had an object lesson in what happens to people who cross the mighty Kanes." Paul's tone was bitter.

"I don't understand."

Paul sighed. "A few minutes after your father left, two guys came in and started a brawl over nothing. They hauled me into it before I could get out of the way, and I ended up in jail. After we were booked, they admitted they'd been paid to do it, by your father."

Arianna gasped. She'd learned so much about her father since his death, and too much of it had hurt.

"While I was in jail, somebody called the police and told them that the *Pelican* was being used for drug smuggling. It was late the next afternoon before I could get that little mess straightened out so I could be released from jail. By then you were gone without so much as a farewell note."

"You had my Denver address and phone number," Arianna murmured, guilt robbing her of any anger.

"When I got home, there was a notice telling me that the mortages on the *Pellington Star* and the Roarke Fishing Camp were now being held by Kane Enterprises. I might have fought him alone, but that fishing camp was all my folks had, and I couldn't risk it. That's when I signed the separation agreement."

"Dear God." Arianna could say nothing else.

"I kept thinking that you'd write or call. I was sure that your father couldn't keep you prisoner forever, but ... Well, after a while, I decided that I'd been wrong."

"But you didn't get a divorce." She spoke softly.

"You never asked for one."

"I never asked for a separation either," Arianna protested.

"You signed it."

"My father said that you'd accepted money, even demanded a payment from him. That was the price of my freedom." Arianna felt tears on her cheeks.

"And you were willing to believe that of me." His tone was hurt and weary.

"I couldn't believe that you'd loved me," Arianna admitted. "I was such a child. Even my father, who claimed that he loved me more than anyone else in the world, assured me that you couldn't have really loved me." She was shaking now, shivering with a cold that came from the sure knowledge of betrayal. "I guess in a way I was right. Leila is much more suitable for you than I ever could be. I don't deserve you."

"Leila?" He sounded shocked.

"She's been here for you, helped you build everything. She has a right to your love, Paul. I shouldn't have come here with you tonight, but I thought I could steal just one more glimpse of what we could have shared, so . . ." Her voice broke, and it was a moment before she could go on. "You and Leila have built a wonderful life together, and now you'll have your freedom."

His fingers touched her face, tracing the damp trail of her tears as gently as a night breeze. She tried not to cry any more, not to let him know what her sacrifice was costing her, but when his other arm slipped around her, she couldn't stop the chills that shook her.

"My poor little love," Paul whispered, drawing her once more against the furry warmth of his chest. "Didn't you know that all of this was built for you? As soon as I realized what your father was doing, I went to work to pay off the mortgages he'd taken over. Once that was accomplished, I started to build the resort. I wanted to be able to offer you the kind of life you deserved, and I wanted to make sure that we'd be financially safe from anything your father might try to do to me."

"But Leila . . ."

"Leila is my friend and partner. She's done a great deal for the resort. If I hadn't had her to run things on the island, I couldn't have spent so much time using the *Pelican* and the *Star* on fishing and tourist trips. But that's all, Arianna. There's never been another woman for me. That's why I never got the divorce your father demanded."

"But you just went to Denver," she reminded him. His hands were moving on her back, stroking her slowly, as though he wanted to memorize every curving hollow and swell of her tingling flesh.

"When I read about your father's death, I thought that you might need me. Then, when I got there, your attorney told me that you'd already left to clear up the matter of getting out of the marriage. He said that you'd asked him for the names of divorce attorneys in this area. He made it clear that you felt that I'd somehow cheated you by not getting the divorce five years ago."

She reached out a hand to trace his beloved features, feeling the feathery movement of his eyelashes against her fingers. "We've wasted so much time."

"We'll just have to make up for it," he told her, and his voice was bubbling with laughter as he sought her lips, his hands moving to more intimate caresses. Her shivers turned to delighted wiggling as she returned his kiss and caresses with joyful abandon.

"Five years of loving could take quite a while," she warned as she felt the surging of his desire and answered it with her own passionate love.

"We have the rest of our lives," he told her as the world faded, leaving only the whirlpool of their passion, the ecstasy of their blazing fulfillment.

The room was growing pale with dawn when Arianna opened her eyes, dimly conscious of the cold on one side of her and the delicious warmth on the other. She snuggled closer, and Paul moaned, his arms enclosing her as memories of the night swept over her.

She sat up abruptly, shocked to look around and see that she was, indeed, still in the cabin. Cold air washed over her as the quilt fell away from her naked body. She tried to pull it up again, but strong hands stopped her.

"Where do you think you're going with my quilt?" Paul demanded, his tone teasingly gruff.

"To the resort," Arianna answered without a great deal of confidence. "People will be wondering . . ." She succumbed to the cold and slid back beneath the quilt.

"Let them wonder," Paul ordered, his hands and lips finding an infinite variety of ways to warm away her shivers and make her forget anything else that might have been on her mind.

Later he sighed and stretched. "I suppose you're right about going back," he admitted, yawning. "This is a dandy bed, but there's nothing to eat here."

Arianna giggled. "Love is fine, but now you're hungry?"

"If we're going to make up for five years apart, I'm going to have to keep my strength up," he warned her.

"You seemed strong enough a few minutes ago," Arianna observed, kissing him with languorous thoroughness.

He groaned, dragged himself away from her, and pitched the quilt onto the old sofa across the room.

"That's cruel," Arianna protested, getting to her feet and fumbling about for her clothing.

Paul nodded, shivering. "We'd starve to death in a warm nest." He paused for a last breath-stealing embrace before pulling on his shirt. "It's time for me to introduce everyone at the resort to my wife."

Arianna swallowed hard, well aware that not all reactions would be happy ones. "Would you like to talk to Leila alone first?" she asked, remembering all the redhead had told her.

"Why?" Paul looked honestly confused. "She already knows about you. I told her the whole story a long time ago, before we went into business together."

Arianna started to protest that he wasn't being fair, then realized with a shock that Paul was truly oblivious of the depth of Leila's feelings. To expose them to him now would be needlessly cruel to Leila. "Let's go," she said.

The announcements went far better than she'd expected. Leila was the first to congratulate them. Her words seemed quite genuine until Arianna looked into her eyes and saw the pain there. The rest of the staff was all smiles and happy words.

Flo offered a hug, whispering, "I thought it might be so when I found your clothes in the lobby."

Breakfast was a champagne celebration shared with the guests. It wasn't until nearly three hours later that Arianna finally found herself alone with Leila in the office. The redhead glared at her. "So you've won," she said.

Arianna forced herself to see the pain beneath the anger. "No, Leila," she answered, "I lost five years that I'll never be able to make up. Years that you shared with Paul in a very special way." She paused, hoping for a response, but Leila's expression was unreadable. "He cares very deeply for you, Leila, and he has no idea how you feel about him," she continued.

"You didn't tell him?" Leila sounded surprised.

Arianna managed a wry smile. "We had enough of our own mistakes to straighten out, Leila. My father did a terribly cruel thing to both of us. I suppose he thought that he was doing what was best for me, but his lies came close to ruining my life, and they hurt Paul dreadfully. I'm only glad that I finally grew up enough to gamble on my own love and come here to face him."

"And what about me?" The animosity was gone, and Arianna could see grudging respect in the hazel eyes that met her gaze squarely.

"That's up to you," Arianna answered. "This resort is partly yours. It's your dream as well as Paul's, and you have every right to enjoy the fulfillment of it."

"What about your dreams?" Leila's tone was tentative.

"The most important one has just come true," Arianna answered. "The rest will grow with the resort—if we can all work together as friends."

Leila studied her for several minutes, then nodded, a slow smile touching her lips. "It was a good five years," she murmured, offering her hand to Arianna, "but I guess I can't lose what I never really had."

At that moment the phone rang beside them and the

bell on the front desk clanged. Arianna's smile changed to a grin. "Which one do I answer?" she asked.

"Get the front desk, I'll take the phone." Leila dropped in the chair beside the typewriter.

Arianna stepped out into the lobby to see that Paul, not a guest, stood on the far side of the desk.

"How is a man supposed to get any service around here?" he demanded. "All the help keeps disappearing."

"I'm sure you'll find a way," Arianna told him as she went around the front desk and into his arms. His kiss told her that no matter what lay ahead, everything was going to work out just fine.

TELL US YOUR OPINIONS AND RECEIVE A FREE COPY OF THE RAPTURE NEWSLETTER.

Thank you for filling out our questionnaire. Your response to the following questions will help us to bring you more and better books. In appreciation of your help we will send you a free copy of the Rapture Newsletter.

1. Book Title:_____

   Book #:_____ (5-7)

2. Using the scale below how would you rate this book on the following features? Please write in one rating from 0–10 for each feature in the spaces provided. Ignore bracketed numbers.

   (Poor) 0 1 2 3 4 5 6 7 8 9 10 (Excellent)
                                        0–10 Rating

   Overall Opinion of Book................. _____ (8)
   Plot/Story............................. _____ (9)
   Setting/Location....................... _____ (10)
   Writing Style.......................... _____ (11)
   Dialogue............................... _____ (12)
   Love Scenes............................ _____ (13)
   Character Development:
   Heroine:............................... _____ (14)
   Hero:.................................. _____ (15)
   Romantic Scene on Front Cover.......... _____ (16)
   Back Cover Story Outline............... _____ (17)
   First Page Excerpts.................... _____ (18)

3. What is your: Education: Age:_____(20-22)

       High School ( )1   4 Yrs. College ( )3
       2 Yrs. College ( )2   Post Grad   ( )4 (23)

4. Print Name:_____

   Address:_____

   City:_____State:_____Zip:_____

   Phone # (   )_____(25)

   Thank you for your time and effort. Please send to New American Library, Rapture Romance Research Department, 1633 Broadway, New York, NY 10019.

RAPTURE ROMANCE

Provocative and sensual, passionate and tender— the magic and mystery of love in all its many guises

NEW Titles Available Now

(0451)

23☐**MIDNIGHT EYES by Deborah Benét.** Noble was as wary of Egyptian men as Talat was of American career women. Could their passion burn through the cultures that bound them? (124766—$1.95)*

24☐**DANCE OF DESIRE by Elizabeth Allison.** Jeffery Northrop offered dancer Patrice Edwards love beyond her wildest dreams—but could she give up her hard-won independence in exchange?

(124774—$1.95)*

25☐**PAINTED SECRETS by Ellie Winslow.** He'd left her four years ago, but now Lawrence Stebbing was back. For Nadine's love—or their son?

(124782—$1.95)*

26☐**STRANGERS WHO LOVE by Sharon Wagner.** Was Paul Roarke really an easily bought-off fortune-hunter? Arianna didn't think so, until her new husband suddenly disappeared . . . (124790—$1.95)*

*Price is $2.25 in Canada

RAPTURE ROMANCE

Provocative and sensual,
passionate and tender—
the magic and mystery of love
in all its many guises

Coming next month

FROSTFIRE by Jennifer Dale. Rachel Devlin thought she only wanted revenge on womanizer Colin Knight. But once she found herself in his arms, her fury turned to desire . . .

PRECIOUS POSSESSION by Kathryn Kent. There was a strength in Max Randolph to which Sabrina Whitfield couldn't help responding. But something warned her to beware, for this ambitious businessman was also her arch rival . . .

STARDUST AND DIAMONDS by JoAnn Robb. Brilliant astronomer Althea Thorne had her gaze fixed on the heavens until baseball star Matt Powers eclipsed all else. But Althea worried that their different worlds would collide and destroy their love . . .

HEART'S VICTORY by Laurel Chandler. Karen Meredith pledged no man would come between her and ballet, until champion skier Erik Nylund melted her icy resistance. But would she have to sacrifice her career for love?

A SHARED LOVE by Elisa Stone. Mark Hager awakened Courtney to an ecstasy she had denied herself. But then she discovered Mark's secret, a secret that could destroy her dreams of love . . .

FORBIDDEN JOY by Nina Coombs. Dynamic physicist Stephen Blackford helped cool New Englander Hester Mather blossom into a confident, beautiful woman. Then he was gone, leaving her to question his love—and to wonder whether the new woman she'd become could win him back. . . .

RAPTURE ROMANCE

Provocative and sensual,
passionate and tender—
the magic and mystery of love
in all its many guises

RAPTURE ROMANCE

**Provocative and sensual,
passionate and tender—
the magic and mystery of love
in all its many guises**

(0451)
# 1	☐	LOVE SO FEARFUL by Nina Coombs.	(120035—$1.95)*
# 2	☐	RIVER OF LOVE by Lisa McConnell.	(120043—$1.95)*
# 3	☐	LOVER'S LAIR by Jeanette Ernest.	(120051—$1.95)*
# 4	☐	WELCOME INTRUDER by Charlotte Wisely.	
			(120078—$1.95)*
# 5	☐	CHESAPEAKE AUTUMN by Stephanie Richards.	
			(120647—$1.95)*
# 6	☐	PASSION'S DOMAIN by Nina Coombs.	(120655—$1.95)*
# 7	☐	TENDER RHAPSODY by Jennifer Dale.	(122321—$1.95)*
# 8	☐	SUMMER STORM by Joan Wolf.	(122348—$1.95)*
# 9	☐	CRYSTAL DREAMS by Diana Morgan.	(121287—$1.95)*
#10	☐	THE WINE-DARK SEA by Ellie Winslow.	(121295—$1.95)*
#11	☐	FLOWER OF DESIRE by Francine Shore.	
			(122658—$1.95)*
#12	☐	DEAR DOUBTER by Jeanette Ernest.	(122666—$1.95)*

*Price $2.25 in Canada

Buy them at your local bookstore or use this convenient coupon for ordering.

THE NEW AMERICAN LIBRARY, INC.,
P.O. Box 999, Bergenfield, New Jersey 07621

Please send me the books I have checked above. I am enclosing $_____
(please add $1.00 to this order to cover postage and handling). Send check
or money order—no cash or C.O.D.'s. Prices and numbers are subject to change
without notice.

Name_____

Address_____

City _____ State _____ Zip Code _____

Allow 4-6 weeks for delivery.
This offer is subject to withdrawal without notice.

SPECIAL $1.00 REBATE OFFER
WHEN YOU BUY
FOUR RAPTURE ROMANCES

To receive your cash refund, send:

1. This coupon: To qualify for the $1.00 refund, this coupon, completed with your name and address, must be used. (Certificate may not be reproduced)

2. Proof of purchase: Print, on the reverse side of this coupon, the *title* of the books, the *numbers* of the books (on the upper right hand of the front cover preceding the price), and the U.P.C. numbers (on the back covers) on your next four purchases.

3. Cash register receipts, with prices circled to:
   Rapture Romance $1.00 Refund Offer
   P.O. Box NB037
   El Paso, Texas 79977

Offer good only in the U.S. and Canada. Limit one refund/response per household for any group of four Rapture Romance titles. Void where prohibited, taxed or restricted. Allow 6–8 weeks for delivery. Offer expires March 31, 1984.

NAME_____

ADDRESS_____

CITY_____STATE_____ZIP_____

SPECIAL $1.00 REBATE OFFER
WHEN YOU BUY
FOUR RAPTURE ROMANCES

See complete details on reverse

1. Book Title _____

Book Number 451-_____

U.P.C. Number 7116200195-_____

2. Book Title _____

Book Number 451-_____

U.P.C. Number 7116200195-_____

3. Book Title _____

Book Number 451-_____

U.P.C. Number 7116200195-_____

4. Book Title _____

Book Number 451-_____

U.P.C. Number 7116200195-_____

U.P.C. Number